MW01245314

Paths:The Diary of Baine Adams

By

Paul Hood

Copyright © 2020 by Paul Hood Published by Willow Moon Publishing
108 Saint Thomas Road
Lancaster, PA 17601 willow-moon-publishing.com
Paths: The Diary of Baine Adams/Paul Hood –1st U.S. Edition
Summary: Paths: The Diary of Baine Adams, is a new take on the classic tale of Cyrano de Begerac. A story that examines the power of words and the mysteries of the human mind and the need to connect with something real.
140 pages ; 229 x 152 mm
Hardcover ISBN-13: 978-1-948256-35-3
1.Fiction/Literary. 2. Fiction/Psychological 3.Fiction/Romance
I. Paths: The Diary of Baine Adams. II. Hood, Paul Printed in the United States on acid free paper
Typeset: Garamond Design by Jodi Stapler

For Grace and Tanaia

"Not all those who wander are lost..." ~J.R.R. Tolkien

By train from Alabama, Baine Henry Adams left for New York City as fast as it appeared in his dreams. He had already bid farewell to familiarities, and with an ambivalent grin and conflicted emotions, was unsure how to wholly revel in his excitement.

As the world passed his peripheral vision in a blur consisting of lush southern landscape, he managed to express the feelings escaping him through the crafting of words in the form of impetuous scribbling in a leather-bound journal he received as a gift from his late mother. "Either you tell me, yourself, or this diary how you feel. No one else needs to know," she'd say.

The pencil-pressed hard against the thick, well-aged pages-were soon consumed with ramblings of anticipated travels toward the northeast. Thoughts materialized like condensation on glass, moisture forming on his mind that trickled into a soul thirsty for wanderlust. With the welling of tears in his eyes due to leaving his childhood home, he could not elude nor erase the visions: hot summer nights with bug-catching and frolicking until exhaustion, which gave way to the greatest of sleep next to a window consumed by an old fan, a fan that brought inward the lukewarm southern air that smelled of plum and peach trees during night.

With the passing of trees and the reddish Alabama earth as the train glided north, glimpses of Momma and her maternal instincts came in vivid flashes. Careful to stifle his emotions from nearby travelers, Baine recalled his acceptance of the sadness that seized him while packing, a difficult task made easy by the thick and comforting scent of cornbread made by Momma that he brought along for comfort. Grandpa, he remembered, had also mastered the recipe and went about creating his own version of the wonderful, golden wedges so he could eat them during Atlanta Braves games.

For Baine, it was soothing memories of writing sessions filled with crumbs falling on paper, butter stains littering wonderful prose and Momma standing in the kitchen clad in a tattered apron, which seemed a comical contrast to her usual brandishing of a lit cigarette dangling from her mouth.

The cornbread was filling, buttered to suit, something Baine knew would stay well on the trip. Thick wedges filled the car with the smell of down home. Baine soon began eating away the memories, redeveloping images of Momma's domestic nature. He could see her facial features: wrinkled and dark, slight and protruding firmly from her face, her mahogany-toned profile, its minimal garishness, and how when facing him, she appeared undeterred and amiable, which often caused him to smile with his mouth full. Momma was comely at first glance. She was never much for smiling as her lips pursed tightly together.

"Baine," she'd say, her southern tongue slippery and thick. "Gon' wash yo hands fo dinna! Time ta eat."

Those were the words she ever knew; words associated with nourishment; other moments were filled with anger, carrying the fierceness of a woman unhinged. Her use of dagger-sharp curse words could puncture the strongest men, catapulting from her mouth like arrows. She was at times a fighting woman. Her soft side rare and unseen most days, came during nights when Baine was tucked away in bed with one eye askew. A calm demeanor that arrived gradually like that of an eclipse, a rare and marvelous thing, would softly intrude upon her personality, shining bright the view of her in a heavenly outline as she stood in the doorway humming church hymns.

The last time Baine had seen Momma, she was dressed for travel. Alongside her leg, a misshapen suitcase bulged as if packed in anger. She was dressed in clothing both heavy and colorful, clothes she wore during the holidays: a forest green sweater too thick for southern weather with lint balls hanging loose against the sleeves, accentuated by a long red scarf eerily resembling an oversized sliver of licorice. Black denim pants covered her legs tightly; her hair was done in the usual bouffant Baine associated with her hosting card games or fish fries. Her perfume was its usual cheap and aromatic bouquet, a floral concoction that lingered throughout the house as though alive. Opening Baine's bedroom door, the morning before leaving for the day, Momma's last words were spoken in a simple tone.

"Mind yo grandpa, ya here?" she said. "Keep them words and dreams a secret til the world is ready or needs them…"

Awakening from a dream in which an old man praised his literary efforts, Baine saw the dimensions of Momma for the last time. She never returned that evening. She never again walked through the door and void was the usual contortion and twisting of features on her face or the usual fussing about something she saw along with other aggravating elements of her day. In her sudden absence from his young life, Baine longed for the oddities contained by her personality; seemed they arrived as cravings, a need for sustenance in the form of love and guidance. One summer evening, he wrote of this while holding back tears:

Momma has gone away without word of return. I am here now with Grandpa. He doesn't talk or sing much like her and I wish he would. Seems he drinks and just watches the world go by throughout the day. He smiles at nothing. Well, seems like nothing. But maybe, like me, he's thinking of Momma too and the good stuff she left for us to think about.

Grandpa was merely a ghost when Momma *was* present—he appeared from the bedroom dressed in what would become a self-imposed uniform of pity over passing months: a tattered white tank-top, stained, blue jean shorts and house shoes old and worn from many years of shuffling feet. Resembling flattened cockroaches, the shoes' shuffling noise made from his slow walk was a warning of his arrival.

"Yo momma still ain't come home?" he'd ask each day.

"No, Pop, not today, she gon. Been gon nearly three months now, you remember?" Baine replied.

"Oh."

Grandpa's response, followed by a distant stare as though trying to remember the last conversation he had with

9

Momma, was coupled later by home-made moonshine made from aged potatoes. The consumption of his creation was unbelievable, a clear display of a need to saturate the memory of Momma's last days at home. Grandpa spent most of his time within the kitchen shirtless, hunched over in a chair with his eyes half-closed with his skin glistening from sweat that glowed under dim kitchen lights.

One day, during the summer of 1992, Baine's already flourishing imagination came upon a vision of a man entering his room. He wasn't a stately being. His skin was dry, his hair was nappy and patched in spots, his nose was overly bulbous and long his body thin. That evening Baine wrote in his diary: *I met a strange man that writes just as I do; he calls himself Cyrano.*

Moonshine brought this demon, Baine thought. In the darkness of his room, he asked with a whisper, "Did Momma send you to watch us?" Numerous questions from Baine followed, filling the house, often going unanswered. The silences allowed ghostly whispers of Momma's voice to resonate, and often, if able to catch a glimpse, Baine could see Grandpa lurking around the house to see if Momma was present.

"Momma Adams," he called. "You home?"

Baine smelled Grandpa's alcohol tinged breath; it was thick and caused grimacing.

"Grandpa," Baine began in protest, "thinkin' you should try'n dry up. Momma will be back, and she won't be happy with your state of being."

Grandpa grunted.

The glazing of Grandpa's eyes shone against the dim light; eyes soon shaded in a permanent red. "Lemme know when she's here," he'd say. "Picked her some flowers from the backyard. She sho do love her some flowers…"

Hearing Grandpa say this brought a sadness Baine could not express through speaking. On a hot summer evening, Baine wrote a simple question to himself:

WHO'S THAT MAN BEHIND THE OTHER MAN I ONCE LOVED…?

Sitting outside of the house beneath the sprawled, gangly branches of his favorite tree that contained the littered remnants of hollowed Cicada casings, Baine would spend hours writing about wanting to shed his life with Grandpa. He wanted to head north to pursue his dream of writing. To live in a city with others that felt and thought the same as he.

One day, during a warm, sunny autumn afternoon, with the air moist and the smell of the nearby steel plant in the neighborhood emitting its strength, the inspiration to journal was more tempting than ever. Baine, discontent with Grandpa's diminishing state, wrote:

I must tell the world that the leaving of Momma has changed my grandpa into a man of unknown habits. One of them is drinking. He drinks a lot, has replaced the common three squares with liquid. I do wish God would talk to him. Does he exist? Is this his way of punishing Momma's conflicted relationship with him? I'm thinking I'll leave soon and maybe try and find momma and see why she left. I guess it's the only way to save Grandpa. Man, has he really turned a bad corner.

It was unnerving, the crumbling of Grandpa. His days had become quite predictable: up to dress, the same clothes from the previous day draping his body along with the scent of drunkenness.

"Momma Adams still ain't come home?" he'd ask.

"No, Pops, not yet, but you best shape up before she comes home. You know how she is when you drink."

A weak grin from Grandpa followed this request.

Disheveled, Grandpa had welcomed untidiness. His hair was kinky and knotted, his face unshaved with matted stubble intermingling with a pock-dented profile that once was smooth and handsome. He was also losing weight, taking on the dimensions of a slight and brown man undone. He remained in his bedroom most evenings, his coarse hair uncombed and brushing against the headboard while he watched countless hours of television. Ever the baseball fan he was, the sounds of the Atlanta Braves from the small, black and white television in his bedroom blared loudly within the house, echoing down the hallway. Light from the television flashed against framed pictures of him and Momma along the wall in an adjacent hallway, revealing much happier days. Days full of laughter and joy and neighborhood girls and boys playing in yards. Baine often watched this happiness while journaling; to capture its truth in all forms, the sensory details of it, the minutiae.

Years had passed, and Baine continued writing about his world, hoping Momma would return. He was now a young man, much wiser than most for his age and further enhancing his writing prowess. The year was 1998; Baine was now a 27-year-old man. He had seen enough of the world before him and it was time to explore his dream of living in the city that never sleeps.

One the night before leaving, Baine sat in his room in a small chair near his bedroom window. With the light low and an incoming breeze that smelled of moist grass and steel, he composed a letter. After finishing, Baine left the note on the kitchen table the morning of October 5, 1998. It was a letter he penned in a hand that seemed not of his own.

"I've returned to help you on your journey," the man said, the silhouette of his prodigious nose visible against the incoming sun. "I'm here if you need the right words. Pleasure to see you after so long."

"Excuse me?"

"You've forgotten me so soon?"

"I'm not sure…"

"You befriended me in your teen years. I help with your compositions when words fail you."

"The words never fail. It's the order of thoughts, feelings that escape me at times."

"Then, I am here. I've always thought a drink to relax seems to get the words to line up correctly."

Baine had the urge to sip Grandpa's moonshine one evening, an act that would change his life. A calming burn within Baine's body, he soon came to love made words flow from the pen with ease.

Grandpa:

I must first offer you an apology. I can never be sure, as you yourself will agree, why Momma has decided to leave us alone. I guess she needed a freedom greater than the surroundings of Bessemer. I'm sure you'll agree: the pipe mill can stifle on many days, and the air hanging above the homes are often covered in gloom. It is assumed the only solace was her providing dinner for us and feeling that we indeed needed her. I guess that can become burdensome after many years, even if it is something she may have viewed as her calling. My guess is we all have them. I hope you find yours, even if it may be the act of making whiskey, the finest in the south I must say so myself. I'll drink to you when I'm up north in the city of New York. I'm going there to pursue my dream of writing and to find Momma. I have just completed the first novel to my liking, and I

13

feel it is ready for publication. It is called The Cornbread Diaries. *It tells of a man documenting his life as a young boy in the south. I know, doesn't sound much like fiction but indeed it is. I managed to separate my own life from the main protagonist, a skill I found very difficult. I wrote it often under the large tree in our front yard. The shade helped my intentions during the summer. Perhaps the fine editors in New York will feel the exhilaration of my creation just as I did when composing it. Anyway, I wish you well and hope that you take care of yourself and moderate your drinking habit. You have some varied spryness left in you; I've seen it during times when the Atlanta Braves were winning. Maybe you should visit Atlanta? Didn't you tell me this is where you lived during your youth? Maybe it's time to go back there? Give my love to the neighborhood and I'll try and write often.*

Love,

Baine

****

Journal entry: September 25th, 2002

I've wished for many months now the words and the story came to life and the thoughts leaped from my mind and danced with me in the night. But I must confess, they were not my words fully. The writing thing, which I have come to know as Cyrano, has crafted the thoughts and feelings that have escaped me; plainly, my arrival in New York was not what I dreamed of as a young man from Alabama. My time here has been rather confusing some days and a year ago it was compounded by an act of hate so unimaginable I felt the city—the world even—would not recover. Now it is hard to find the things that inspired me. All I do now is drink with Cyrano and he tells me what I need to write (or what to say sometimes) and I'm hating every minute of it. I want out of this. I know I do.

Baine had not written those words to a woman by the name of Sorena Lopez. Unable to convey such feeling toward another woman as a young man while living in Bessemer, the act of the "writing thing" named Cyrano had returned yet again; and Cyrano was quite vigilante. The words from the writing thing's pen were richer than ever for first drafts, and there was an amount of humbling genius unfathomable to Baine when reading the remarkable composition.

He stared again at the salutation.

Sincerely,

Cyrano…

"It's not a good thing," Baine mumbled. "You coming to New York…not good at all. I would appreciate if you left for good."

He was expecting a response, but there was none. There were only sounds of New York's East Village: the relentless horns of scorned cabbies, the chattering residents walking about the human-cluttered streets; the passing of an ambulance.

Walking toward his living room window to confirm his vision, there was the emission of a gasp as his eyes came across four handprints staining the window with a transparent smudge.

Please leave me…!

"Why are you so scared to approach this woman?" Cyrano said. "Why are you deathly afraid of her beauty?"

"Not gonna listen to you," Baine growled.

Cyrano began the recitation of words written hours before his unwanted return.

"Sorena, meet me at the gate…"

Baine covered his ears, began pacing the room frantically.

"…The one with the lions and gargoyles. It's on Daisy Avenue…"

"Leave, now!" Baine yelled.

"…Is there such a place known as Daisy Avenue in the city, Baine?"

Baine paused. He removed his hands from his ears.

"I'm not…"

"Please wear the dress with the spaghetti straps that kiss your shoulders lovingly as they lie atop your wonderful…"

"Enough, Cy…!"

The room was now quiet.

Walking toward his kitchen table, Baine began searching for his note pad in which he was soon scribbling in a frantic script:

I WISH YOU'D FIND THE COURAGE…

"Perhaps it would be better for you to write a letter like this," Cyrano began. "One that should read as…..

"Since my arrival to the city I have thought of you often; I have imagined your presence on the subway heading north toward uptown. From our meeting, I have not been able to pull my eyes away from the remaining burn in my psyche left by your powerful brightness. There are no limits as to the wonderful words that one can use to describe you. But within my letter, for the time being, I'll choose two: Beautiful. Striking. I feel on many days your aura is the equivalent of a solar eclipse; that I'm only to take in your view with the covering of sunglasses. This is due to your heavenly outline, and it is necessary to adorn the protective eyewear so one may stubbornly stare into your world and maybe your life

as well. As for now, I think I will remain affixed, watching closely your delicate and precise moves through New York's autumn. Stay as you are. I will send you another letter in one day; the day the moon is full above Earth."

He had suddenly appeared in the corner of Baine's apartment. He was well dressed and smiling; his clothes a blur. Nonetheless, it was enough. Baine could smell his earthy odor. He was back at a most inopportune time.

"You'd be better off facing yourself," Cyrano uttered. He was glaring at his fingernails.

"Doing this my way," Baine said.

"You think she'll be there, waiting...Waiting for you?"

Baine sighed.

He hoped she'd be there as the same woman, and he could not go one minute without thinking of her.

"I must tell you you're missed in Georgia," Cyrano said, gazing at his fingernails.

"Not sure why you would say that," Baine said. "Um not even from Georgia."

"I'll let you keep that thought. Fun seeing you go on like nothing's wrong."

"Whatever!"

A gentle breeze came inside from the city. Inhaling deeply, he enjoyed the smell of city life. It was a better odor than the writing thing from the south, an aroma far better indeed.

B

Baine, on the F heading north and away from his apartment in Greenwich Village on November 5, 2002, was allotted a view that seemed to siphon the air from his being. She materialized from nowhere, pushing her way smoothly through a crowd of men and women not nearly as breathtaking or alluring in her immediate presence. During her fruition, Baine's feverish journaling was halted. His new entry, the first that came with interruption since his arrival in New York, read as this:

Entry: Train ride uptown from Greenwich Village toward 110 Street, Cathedral parkway. First time on the F train: scared and excited at the same time.

On such machinery, I feel I'm being followed. This immense iron worm traveling through granite guts of a megapolis has conjured a great sense of paranoia upon me. There are many people on board, none of them as dark as me or dressed the same. Most are wearing suits. I wish they knew who I was or why I was here. Most would not care though. There are many stories on their faces. Cyrano has decided to follow me; his face

18

scares me, like Grandpa's face when he was angry, those harsh reddened
eyes intermingling with a weathered and dented hate for life.

She boarded from 34th street near Herald Square, and her
beauty was striking. The muffled voice of the train technician
murmured over the echoed sound of shuffling feet, "Keep
away from the closing doors, please. Next stop…42nd Street-
Bryant Park."

A man dressed in a tailored, navy blue suit stood next to
her, his free hand holding the balance bar above him. In his
other hand, he held a cellular phone pressed firmly against his
ear. When done, he closed his phone, sighed, and pushed his
long, dark hair back. *Is she with him?* Baine thought. He could
no longer continue taking in the strange man's presence while
basking in the nagging thoughts. He became invisible. *She* was
what he dreamed of when developing images of women in
Manhattan. With a tall, long body—nice in proportion—
ascending toward a face adorned with features dark and
exotic. Her eyes were dark brown and sitting behind a calm
face with comely features. Her thick lips were subtly covered
with clear gloss and when she smiled, her teeth were
adequately straight and fitting to her face. Her only flaw was
that of a small dimple on her right cheek. Baine assumed she
was either Hispanic or Greek due to her dark raven-toned
hair that was straight and he could only imagine smelled
wonderful when swept by an intrusive breeze. Her aura
would not be hindered by the natural odors of SOHO. She
could not blend with the smell of urine, soured trash, and the
warm, oily scent of the subway system or pizza parlors. She
looked like a transplant from the outer boroughs, Brooklyn
perhaps. She was too refined for Queens and presented

19

Bowery coolness with Greenwich Village confidence while exuding an aura of Upper East Side privilege.

Baine hoped she was not a high-price escort.

With his eyes toward his journal, there was only one last thing he could document before closing the cover:

MY GOODNESS....

No way she'll sit next to me, Baine thought. *Plenty of other seats...*

Baine was unaware of the unoccupied seat next to him and the woman was already near: she appeared spent. On her forehead was a lone lock of hair clinging to mild perspiration.

"Excuse me," she said. "May I...?"

Baine was frightened by her beauty. He kept his eyes downward.

"Ma'am?" Baine drawled.

The woman furrowed her brow.

She smiled, sat down next to him, and the smell of her was just as he imagined: an aroma of vanilla, subtle and teasing.

Baine glanced gingerly at her legs. She was indeed a New Yorker. Her impressive calves, olive-colored and muscle-toned from city walking grazed slightly the top of knees shiny and soft in appearance. Her ankles were slightly bruised with a band-aid placed over a small cut.

Crossing her legs, the woman turned toward Baine, smiling.

Baine turned away, opened his journal, and wrote in a cryptic script:

And she is the elusive woman of dreams...?

"Never thought I'd be doing this," she mumbled. "Back on the F train again..."

"Ma'am?"

"I was just saying I haven't been on this train in months."

The woman flipped her hair. Baine inhaled. He decided to take in her existence, fully.

"My first time," Baine said.

"You're kidding?"

"No, been here for years, just never had the patience to wait for the F," Baine said. He wanted his voice to dispose of the nervous tremor. "Name's Baine, Baine Adams," he added, extending his hand as he anticipated her touch. The train pulled away from the stop and the slight jolt caused Baine to gently lurch forward.

"I'm Sorena," she said, softly.

Shaking hands with Sorena, Baine could not help but notice her skin was softer than anything he'd ever felt

"Nice to meet you," Sorena said.

"Likewise."

"You're not from here, are you?"

"No, Alabama. Bessemer, a small town, a suburb of Birmingham."

Sorena pulled a face.

"You moved here by yourself?"

"Umm...Yeah."

"Brave..."

The train began to slow, the ominous clanging sound from the tracks beneath reduced to a hum as an upcoming tunnel cascaded the train in temporary darkness. Baine hoped this was not one of his lost dreams. Pulling inside the terminal, there was the illumination of passengers waiting and it was enough to bring him back. He did not want the moment to end. He thought of staying on the train and venturing as far as he could in hopes that Sorena was doing the same. She was looking at her watch. Baine noticed her crossed leg was shaking. *She's in a rush*, he thought.

"So, what really brought you here," Sorena asked.

"Need an experience," Baine said.

"Experience?"

"Well, a New York experience, I guess."

"Well you keep riding the B and you'll get it," Sorena said with a slight giggle. "Especially during Baseball season; Yankee fans can be characters," she added.

"Works for my profession then."

"That is…"

"I dabble in the art of fiction."

"Hmm…You're a writer?"

Baine nodded. The train buckled gently when hitting a corner. It then came to a stop within a terminal: "42nd Street-Bryant Park…" The doors slid open. A small horde of passengers scurried for the exit, and new arrivals entered. "Well," Sorena said, adjusting her skirt, "welcome to New York."

Baine decided it would be in his interest to ask of Sorena's origins. But he wanted to wait; the train began moving and he was leery about the weird silence. People stood silent within subway cars; it was that one place where New York was, at times, oddly serene. "Where you from, may I ask?"

"Oh," Sorena appeared surprised. "From Queens."

"Queens?"

"Born and raised."

"Oh," Baine mumbled, wishing he had a snappy New Yorker's dialect. He wanted then to know where Sorena was going. *How much time do I have?* he thought.

22

"Anyway, Umm…"

"It's Baine."

"Sorry, really bad with names…"

"It's fine…"

"…What will you do with yourself after you get your 'experience?'"

Sorena made air quotes.

Baine looked down at his journal, surveyed his scribbled text: MY GOODNESS…

"Maybe I'll try the west coast?"

"Have I read any of your work?"

"Not sure," Baine said, gaining a suitable comfort level. "My latest was published by a small press…"

"The title?"

"*The Cornbread Diaries.*"

"Hmm…Nice title."

"It's sort of a memoir, if you will."

"Oh, nice. Are you working on anything now?"

The train buckled again. Baine wondered why no one appeared concerned.

"Well your memoir sounds interesting," Sorena said. "I like the title. It's funny how a good title can attract readers. I happen to read a lot."

Delighted by her interest Baine hated the word "interesting". It was never something he appreciated hearing within writer circles.

"Thanks," Baine mumbled.

"Well, maybe your latest is a romantic work?" Sorena asked.

"Guess I should bone up on my romantic experiences then," Baine said, wishing he hadn't uttered such a statement.

"Seriously?" Sorena said with an inquisitive tone. "A handsome man like you won't have any trouble here in the city."

Baine smiled.

"Thanks for the encouragement. Not many girls where I come from."

Sorena's tightened posture had loosened, and her arms and legs—which were previously crossed—had opened up as if she were a flower in full bloom. Desperate, Baine wanted his mouth to say the words developing in his mind. He soon settled for secretive documentation of desires.

Opening his journal his he scribbled in small letters:

You're so beautiful, oh how I would send you spinning with the love I'd feel for you. The kinetic energy from countless hours of my powerful dreams of your luscious form would move us through the earth's time. Never would you not hear or feel my love.

It was not long before her stop came. The train began to slow down, entering the terminal at Spring Street. The horde of commuters from the deepest parts of Long Island and beyond began making their way toward the doors. With the arrival of others as the doors opened, Baine could smell the heat rising from beneath the train. It mixed with the smell of autumn and lives moving away from him. Sorena stood up, her face still soft and contemplative.

"It was very nice to meet you," Sorena said.

"Nice to meet you as well," Baine replied.

Sorena turned and walked toward the door. It closed as soon as she exited—as though life had resumed for her. Baine had quickly forgotten where he was going, and he wanted the connection to last. As the train pulled away, his last vision of her was her ascending the stairs. Her presence was soon blocked by the fruition of commuters coming down toward the metro stand.

He wondered if he'd see her again.

Tonight, at the strike of seven, we will meet...

The sun shone brightly through large bay-window. Baine crouched at a corner table within his kitchen- had taken to journaling within his leather-bound notebook. Pressing hard atop the stenographer notepad, he was often prone to tearing through the thin sheets. Frustration began building because of Cyrano's unwarranted return; his presence came without much warning.

How I could have possibly forgotten this mad man, Baine thought.

Having halted his writing, Baine crumpled the sheet in front of him, tossing the remains of his thoughts beneath his chair. The wads of paper on the floor resembled a paper graveyard.

A nearby window—still open from last evening—brought along an uninvited breeze.

It's Cyrano... Baine thought.

He rode in on the air most times. Baine could soon hear him breathing.

"Having trouble, I see," Cyrano said. He appeared delighted; he gathered a long look at the table, running his curious eyes along the spine of a thick biography containing a picture of Stanley Kubrick on its cover.

"What, you wanna read?" asked Baine.

Cyrano shrugged. His shoulders made an odd, cracking sound.

"If I didn't write it, why bother," Cyrano said.

"Whatever," said Baine. "Your arrogance will get you nowhere in this town."

"My arrogance got you published, kiddo."

"Do not ever in your life call me kiddo!"

Cyrano smiled, began shaking his head. Pulling a chair away from the table, he sat down with a thud.

Baine could smell Cyrano's movements.

"That book you're leaning over is about a brilliant man, a filmmaker ahead of his time."

Cyrano ran his finger along the cover.

"Does this man have anything to do with the woman you met on the train?" Cyrano asked.

"No Cy, please. Make this visit a short one; I have work to do."

Cyrano waved his hand.

"Whatever, look, let's just get the letter done so we can meet this woman. I mean really *meet* her. Your timid behavior towards women of quality astounds me."

Baine shrugged.

"Maybe I'm thinking too much," Baine mumbled.

"… Or maybe you feel horribly guilty for following her home last evening…" Cy said to himself, as if ashamed. Baine stared hard at Cy.

"I did nothing of the sort," Baine said.

"Your memory, elusive as a Georgia June Bug."

"I stayed on the train. I know I did."

Baine could not imagine he followed such a woman; an image of a wandering butterfly came to him, its delicate wings fluttering through the teeming vistas of Manhattan as it soon came to land at the home of Sorena, a rare and beautiful lady not to be seen by his wanting eyes ever again. He was sure the moment was fleeting, a lovely dream so vivid his five senses allotted the moment to play out fully formed.

Cyrano broke the memory of this with his relentless goading.

"You do want her to fall madly in love with you, right?" said Cyrano.

"Yes of course, but on my terms. Not yours."

"Perhaps you should have a drink to calm your intentions?"

Looking toward the whisky bottle—which sat untouched for several days—Baine noticed it was no longer gleaming under fall sunlight and had accumulated dust.

I *SHOULD WRITE FROM MY HEART, HE'S RIGHT…*

"You're so smart, maybe you should write to her. I can't seem to pull together what I want to say."

"I am quite versed in the art of love it would seem."

"No time for smugness. Cy…here, take the paper, write!"

****

Dr. Herman Stanton hated New York; his southern aptitude left him quite unsettled while walking the busy streets of Manhattan and he vowed never to walk them again. Inside a cab heading toward his hotel room on the Upper East Side, he was reading over notes from previous sessions conducted with one Henry Baine Adams. A nice, calm man, Baine was unlike any other patient Dr. Stanton worked with during his twenty-five-year tenure. His meekness bordered feminine, his voice soothing, nearing a subtlety as though there was something hidden behind his words, as though another person was telling him to remain in such a disposition and his intelligence was far beyond the realm of an average man afflicted with a mental illness called DID (Dissociative Identity Disorder).

Flipping a page in his notebook, Dr. Stanton glared cautiously toward the rearview mirror and saw the cabbie's harsh glare. He was a man of an unknown ethnicity to Dr. Stanton; one he would not have cared about unless he was analyzing his behavior.

His studying glance was cold.

The elements that made New York were far more unhinged than the evident tightness of the south. Dr. Stanton surmised Baine developed a new persona to fit in amongst the quickness of the northeast. He feared Baine had already "switched" due to trauma from childhood. Dr. Stanton did not know much about Baine's birth parents; he was only familiar with a woman Baine often referred to as, "Momma," a tough lady Baine mentioned, "only nice to me at night. She sang songs to me while I lay in bed."

Hearing Baine's memory of those nights with Momma, Dr. Stanton imagined Baine adorned with clothes too small for his elongated body, alone and writing inside a notebook, forming words already impressive and coherent, a protégé of mass talent at such a feeble time. There was no hint of a problem until one afternoon when it was witnessed—with astonishment—Baine had written the words inside of his notepad as someone else.

"This writing thing tells me to say this stuff," he drawled.

"What thing?" Dr. Stanton asked.

"His name is Cyrano," Baine said. "Won't let me sleep. He comes in from outside at night, through the window in my room."

"You ever think it might be that you have a great imagination?"

"No, cuz he tells me I'm *not* anything without him."

Dr. Stanton remembers the long silence, the ominous echoing sound of the clock on his desk. A few minutes pounded by and he was sitting in front of an ingenious man with a complex mental disorder.

"Tell me more about the writing thing," Stanton asked, scribbling his theories.

Baine's posture appeared curled, as if he was holding something between the folds of his stomach.

"Baine?" Stanton inquired.

He remembers how he'd lose Baine. It appeared he escaped himself for hours, remained lost in the "writing thing's" world of distant pleasures and synopsis. Upon his return, he craved the calming effects of alcohol, an odd habit at his young age.

"Writing a book?" the cabbie asked. His eyes now were soft, inquisitive.

"Just getting some work together," Stanton said.

"Kinda work?"

"I work in mental health."

The cabbie made a hard turn, scowled.

"You're in the right city for your line of work," the cabbie said.

Dr. Stanton smiled.

****

A random, undated note found in Baine Adams' apartment:

I can't remember what day it is, so I'll begin to write about my previous night. I met a man that made me think of you. He was ashamed by an event in which his wife had succumbed. The event was a wretched act. It was infidelity. You may ask yourself why I would associate such an act of contempt toward you. But I must say listening to this strange man and hearing of his pain made me want you in my life more than ever.

Cy

Baine, hungover from drinking, was greeted by the presence of Cyrano who had not left since the previous night. Cyrano's grotesque form was hunched over as he was quietly reading a book. Baine wondered what book he mentioned reading last if he had mentioned any at all and to whom he had spoken with while in a drunken state.

"Good morning," Cyrano mumbled, not turning to face Baine.

Baine ignored the statement. He was too sick to acknowledge the greeting.

"Hey…" Baine began, stoically.

"You look like shit," Cyrano said.

"…Were you with me last night?" Baine asked.

"Certainly," Cyrano said. "Cause for celebration, remember?"

"I don't remember anything."

"I do. You were talking about this book to some man at the bar," Cyrano said, running his finger over the book cover.

"What are you talk'n about?"

"This…"

Pulling the book from the table Cyrano held it up toward the side of his face. The cover was black and there was no author name or title.

Baine suddenly felt nauseous. The relief of a bubbling belch arrived.

Cyrano giggled.

"That's not any book of mine," Baine said, grimacing.

"I was doing it for you," Cyrano said, smiling. "You still drink the cheap stuff when we go out; you know you almost ordered a glass of Boone's Farm?"

"I only drank Grandpa's moonshine."

"Well, you almost ordered that crap for us last night."

I would never drink cheap wine…

"Whatever I do outside of here and with you is strictly for research on my next book," Baine said, staring at the book Cyrano was reading. He sifted through his memory of the evening:

The bartender…?

Some guy smoking a cigar at the bar.

A disinterested Asian woman leaving…No she was a white lady, blonde…No, wait…. A redhead, shoulder-length hair. She smiled at me…

"No use trying to remember," said Cyrano. "You all but stood up and sang about the damn thing in there. It's our secret. I wish you would have listened to what I was saying. You never listen!"

Baine's stomach growled.

That must be my anthology, he thought.

"Hey, that's my book of poems!" Baine shouted.

"Oh, you've figured it out," Cyrano began, his voice cracking. "You have the nerve to call me insecure, ha! You should read some of these things."

"Those are from years ago!"

"Nothing's changed, has it?"

"Huh?"

"You still act like you're better than all of us because you have a gift for language."

"That's insane!"

"Insanity is lying about the fact you don't have a drinking problem, which you gave to both of us and you're drinking yourself into a stupor at a bar for research. That's insane!"

Baine became quiet.

"You're just like me," Baine said, placing his hand on his stomach while grimacing.

"No, I'm not scared of love and beauty like you."

"And that means...?"

"Sorena?"

"This has nothing to do with her!"

"You're scared of rejection, so you hide behind the swimmin' bliss, right?"

How's he know that saying....?

"You have no idea what you're talking about," Baine said.

"She likes me better anyway."

"Whatever. Think what you want. My work as a writer has to lead to something in this city, even if it's rejection by some girl I encountered on the train."

"I wish you'd gain the courage..." Cyrano groaned, his eyes glaring.

Baine could not remember where he had heard this saying before. The room became quiet. Cyrano shifted his presence toward the couch.

"Anyway, what's in it for you?" Cyrano asked.

Baine slumped against the wall and slid toward the floor.

"I just wanna know," Baine began. "Wanna know if my writing can touch someone, anyone!"

"Well, you did what I asked," Cyrano said. "Time will tell."

****

Voice recorded documentation: Herman L. Stanton PHD.

"There's seems to be a new development with patient Baine Adams, patient number five-six-two-three-seven-

zero from the Georgia state mental hospital. I would go as far as to assume this is a case of what is known as Dissociative Fugue. Seems he has wandered from the facility suddenly and forgotten much of his past life. He has become a man that lives and works in New York. Oddly enough he has used something from his original personality as the basis: his writing. He has allowed the entity known as the writing thing to help him adjust. Further examination will help me to understand the new personality. I need to find out if another personality can mimic the host's persona and use the natural ability of the host to create an unspecified reaction. Baine has always been my most complex subject. His past has caused him to split into several other interesting personalities. And now, it seems one of them is destined to find answers to how its existence came to fruition."

Baine, tonight I think you should write this one for yourself.
Remember, try not thinking too hard. Write from your heart. Please
leave the "purple" stuff and mechanics to me. Well, good luck! Anyway,
I think Sorena would appreciate your efforts.

Cyrano was standing in the middle of Baine's living room. It seemed the letter he'd written consumed endless amounts of time. There was an attempt to fathom why Baine could not complete the task on his own. *He may well screw this up; he does not have what it takes to convey his deepest emotions. Poor kid, such a lost...*

Holding the letter, Cyrano had not noticed it fell from his hand. He could do nothing but watch the letter float away from him and land on the floor to reveal its scribbled contents. "Nothing left..." he mumbled, realizing his presence was fading upon the air of the day. With an approaching sadness, Cyrano walked away from the living room. He did not want to see his inevitable disappearance.

Alone in the kitchen, Baine considered Grandpa's whiskey. It was now hidden inside the cool, darkness of an unused cupboard. The stove was clean, untouched as usual. Baine never made dinner, it seemed. There was an attempt to regain his previous strength. He could almost hear—across the hall—Cyrano mumbling, "Sure would like to eat."

Opening the oven door on the stove, there was the discovery of Boone's Farm wine. Baine smiled, removed the bottle and quickly grabbed a glass from the sink.

He did not bother with washing it clean.

The pouring of thick wine enveloped the clear glass, filling its circumference in a soft, vermillion shade. Baine associated this vision—aided by a beam of sunlight coming through the kitchen window—with his encounter with Sorena. Thoughts or days when he had seen her with his eyes. Those days when the sun did not shine and the B train left the 34th Street stop, heading toward Upper Manhattan where its distant rays came through intrusive clouds when Sorena appeared. Her dark hair was illuminated. Her scent rushed through the stale air, cutting through toward his senses. He wondered often if anyone else could smell her because he wanted to own her aroma.

Leaving this selfish wish behind, Baine moved the glass toward his dry lips. Sipping slowly, there was contemplation of writing. With his chest warmed by the swallowing of cheap wine, Baine approached his writing desk. Sitting down, he stared blankly at the pen and pad before him.

...Honestly, is there ever a way I could be as good as Cyrano? he thought. *How can I possibly...?*

Baine recalled Cyrano's advice:

Tonight, I think you should write this one for yourself. Remember, try not thinking too hard. Write from your heart. Please leave the "purple" stuff and mechanics to me. Well, good luck! Anyway, I think Sorena would appreciate your efforts.

Holding the pen between his fingers, Baine smiled. He recalled how much of the act of writing he enjoyed. Confined by solitude, the act was far more enjoyable than he assumed. There was no longer fear of judgment or criticism. There was readiness for the unknown. Gone was fear.

* * * * * * * *

Dr. Stanton had not changed his clothes since arriving in New York. Standing in front of the bathroom mirror in his hotel room, he could hear the distant, echoed opinion of his wife: "You should probably pack a few more things to wear, you never know..."

On board the plane he avoided thinking of luggage. He had enough to worry him. Baine Adams in particular would take up most of his thoughts. *I was thinking it'd be easy to get him to come back*, Dr. Stanton thought. It was easy before. Severity realigned everything he once knew about his sessions with Baine. Dissociative Fugue had arisen unexpectedly.

Stanton began researching a list of publishers within Manhattan. Unless there was employment somewhere such as a restaurant or driving a cab, the possibility of living well was far removed. There would have been the need to list former employers and previous addresses. His social security number would have revealed enough to lead prospective employers toward the discovery he indeed was a patient sought by Georgia State Hospital.

With his clothes removed, Dr. Stanton thought he should have listened to his wife, something he had done over the passing years. He was more prone to rehash the distracting numerations offered by Baine—listening to his proliferations with great intent, taking in his words and documenting them verbally on his hand-held tape recorder. Becoming less enthralled by his wife's one-dimensional behavior, her gentle nagging, and sudden inquisitions intermingling with a passive-aggressiveness both odd and petulant, was now a bore. Gone was Stanton's craving for stability and companionship he once longed for while proverbially sauntering through college. He enjoyed the complexities of mental illness; enjoyed the unanswered questions and theories, the mysteries of the mind, the multitude of intricacies.

On the phone with a publisher, he was greeted by a receptionist.

"Marchen and Stark, how can I assist you?"

"Uh…yes," Stanton began, "I'm looking for an editor or someone that can help me with information about an author named Baine Adams."

There was a moment of uncomfortable silence.

"Hello?" Dr. Stanton said.

"Uh, one moment, your name again?" the receptionist asked.

"Herman Stanton, Dr. Herman Stanton."

The hold music wasn't what he expected: an old David Bowie song he hadn't heard since his childhood.

"Hello?"

"Yeah, may I ask whose calling?" a voice said. It was a male. He sounded as if he were chewing.

Dr. Stanton sighed, thought of his wife, and her advice about clothes. He wished she would have mentioned how New Yorkers talked.

"This Dr. Stanton; I'm calling to get information about one of your authors. The name's Baine Adams. He wrote a book you published called *The Cornbread Diaries*?"

"Hmm…Baine…Adams. Not sure I recognize the name. We're a small press, I'm sure I'd have recognized a name like Baine."

A muffled voice came from the background.

"Just looked it up online, it's self-published. Good reviews though."

"Oh, that book?" the man began. "Someone was telling me about it the other day. Said it's really good for a self-published work."

"So, you do know him?" Stanton inquired.

"Yeah, umm…just the name, not much else; we get a slew of unsolicited manuscripts; we keep our distance and just help put the books together. We're pretty much a vanity publisher; we tell this in very clear terms to our authors upfront. We do everything in house, unlike companies like say, Ingram."

Dr. Stanton found himself remembering sessions with Baine, and how he spoke of Cyrano, Cyrano the "writing thing." He was like the character from the tale of *Cyrano De Bergerac*, a persuasive personality who smelled funny and had a long nose. He was from…

Dr. Stanton forgot he was on the phone, distracted by a distant subliminal thought…

"That writing thing came into my room again last night…"

"Dr. Stanton…?"

"I'm not sure if you heard me. But yeah, we're not what you would call a traditional publisher; we kinda help people who want to self-publish. Basically, we do vanity…."

"So, you've heard of this book and the author is what you're saying?"

"Yes, a colleague of mine was raving about the book just the other day."

"Do you pay royalties?"

"It depends on..."

The man paused. Continuing, he asked, "You're not really with triple B, are you?"

"Excuse me?" said Stanton.

The man disconnected the call.

Half-naked and probing a small vanity publisher in New York was not the way he wanted to spend his time in Manhattan. Stanton brought to memory Baine's look of bewilderment when approaching him near Central Park. It was as if he knew of him and wanted his presence to slowly disintegrate. There was a moment of awful waiting, a moment when all things surrounding them disappeared, and there they both stood, surveying each other's existence with nothing in motion but the inhaling of autumn air and the stifled exhalation of questions between them. They had not seen nor heard from one another until the act of switching infiltrated what was deemed as progress. Dr. Stanton recalled his sudden shock when Baine simply stated, "Funny, right? Me living in New York..."

There was nothing uncomfortable or dishonest about his statement. He was not in another place in his mind or inhabited by the personality of Cyrano.

He said this with great sincerity as Baine.

****

There was beautiful darkness over Manhattan. Aided by Cyrano, Baine finished writing the next letter he would give to Sorena. He finished them while drunk on Grandpa's whiskey. He had passed out while working, awakened only once as himself. His face was lined with a dried string of drool and was horribly indented with the markings from his writing table. He thought of how ridiculous he must have looked due to the habit of sleeping with his eyes open while they twitched from the act of R.E.M. He was not one to indulge in the act of sleeping in odd places. Switching, he knew, would cause him to lay wherever the personality felt comfortable, and the consequences would be a night in jail or him being shipped back to the R.T.F.

Awakening as himself, Baine resumed life, arriving home at midnight. Entering his apartment, he could smell the odor of cheap wine and sweat. He thought of Cyrano and rubbed his face. Walking over toward the couch, he mumbled under his breath, "Get up, you lazy bastard."

"I finished the letter, and this is how you repay me?" Cyrano said.

Moving his body on the couch, Cyrano's scent was unbearable. Baine shook his head.

"Well, I hope you managed to get it done being that you're drunk...again."

"Pa's shine is...how'd...he says...swimmin' bliss? Geez he was such a country fuck. Remember his hair....?"

Baine walked away.

The tone and structure of the note revealed when Cyrano drank, he was a better writer. Misspellings and grammatical flaws littered the pages, but within its mess, the content was rich and bubbled on the page.

Great, Baine thought, if only he wasn't drunk...

Interrupted by the sound of rustling from the couch, there was the faint sound of footsteps. Toward the living room Baine went, removing himself from the examination of Cyrano's letter. Listening intently, the painful noise of a man vomiting was heard.

Baine winced.

He hadn't heard such a sound since leaving Bessemer. It was the same awful wretch Grandpa made after drinking too much moonshine.

"Cyrano?"

The sour odor of cheap wine wafted through the apartment.

"Cyrano, are you...?"

He considered the question useless.

"Go away, Baine." Cyrano slurred.

Baine imagined Cyrano's words as liquid.

"Won't say 'I told you so...'"

One last spit from Cyrano; then the whirling sound of a flushing toilet.

"That'll teach you to drink cheap homemade booze," Baine said, gloating.

Gurgling, Cyrano replied with a mumble, "I suggest you say nothing and worry about yourself."

"You should stick to writing, leave the drinking to me."

"Don't counsel me, kiddo."

Baine shook his head.

"Make sure you clean up good."

The drunkenness was enough to awaken passionate words. Sauntering back toward the kitchen, he could not help but feel an amount of sadness. On the table a pen, notepad, and his old typewriter sat, waiting. Its discovery was suitably illuminated by soft moonlight coming through the kitchen window. Beside his tools for writing: an empty bottle of Boone's Farm. He wondered when Cyrano had time to purchase it. Grandpa was a heavy drinker for most of his life; he was a man controlled by the dizzying sensation of his own liquid happiness. He was much different when sauced: insightful, talkative, gentle. He was a man of useless information and wit; the charm oozed from reddened, glassy eyes and flushed skin. Along with his rugged appearance, there were the disjointed trimmings of a man with soul and compassion.

Growing older, Baine discovered Grandpa's need for drinking; seemed he sipped whiskey not for enjoyment, but to create the man he once was within himself. He talked to anyone listening; he would talk to kids that played in their bare feet with dry thoughts in their minds. He was indeed what he began calling his moonshine, the swimmin' bliss of a man, a war vet who had loved many women and was from Mississippi, a crawl-dad catchin' fool from the south who never came home until dusk during summer. He was brilliant when three sheets to the wind, a storyteller like Faulkner, a man who told of great tales without penning a single letter.

Breaking from the memory of Grandpa, the water running from the faucet in the kitchen reminded Baine of the creek behind his childhood home, where the smells of wet grass and earth were strong, and if listening closely, he could hear the mating call of bullfrogs across the low-trickling water.

This dream oasis within his psyche was a place for escape: wondrous and green with an orange sky from a slow setting sun and crickets chiming in the distance. Cicada's joined the symphony of nature, and there was nothing that could pull Baine away, nothing but the emergence of a damning presence—Cyrano—and he emerged from the bathroom with hopelessly glazed eyes. Pale and lethargic, he smelled of sweat and rye.

Wiping his mouth, Cyrano groaned.

"I don't mean to lecture you," Baine began, "but Grandpa seemed to waste his life drinking, you know?"

"Don't worry about me," Cyrano said.

"We have to help each other."

"I said don't worry!"

"Who else will?"

Cyrano made a face.

"My job is to make you sound better, that's all!"

"But you have to drink to do that. That's a shame!"

"Whatever works."

Saying nothing, Cyrano waved his hand. He began walking back toward the couch. From the living room came the filtered mumbling of his voice: "You seem to be taking your frustrations out on me because you don't have words for Sorena."

Baine replied, "She'll never love a drunkard."

Grabbing the empty bottle from the table, Baine held it up, waving it in front of his face. "It's all gone," he said. "See, this'll get us nowhere. She's too sophisticated for this."

Cyrano laughed, a wet cackle coming from his belly.

"You need to stop, seriously."

"One more word of my having a drinking problem and I'll stop the letters. And you know Sorena will never know how you really feel cuz you're a big coward."

Baine did not respond.

"I'm serious. No more booze."

"So predictable, just like Grandpa, you're even starting to look like him. Things get a little rough and you push away what's important."

"All I ask is that you try writing when sober, okay?"

"Like swimmin' bliss…!"

Cyrano began laughing hysterically.

Baine frowned, feeling his grip on the bottle tighten. He wanted to throw it.

"Look," Cyrano began, coughing from his fit of laughter. "Look at me! Look at this! I forget I'm ugly. I forget no one loves me. I forget about loneliness. I forget there are three million people in this city, and no one is here for me. So, kiddo, you can take your Boy Scout routine to the mountains and jump off a fuckin cliff. Don't destroy my…."

Cyrano was gone.

Baine, coming back to himself, had discovered the empty bottle of Boone's Farm Wine in his hand. There was nothing he could say; nothing to chase away the discovery. He was drunk, angry, and sick. He was the man he scolded, the man he did not want to become. "Tomorrow I write sober," Baine said. "It's the only way."

E

Sorena's childhood friend Dean worked for the Brown Agency. Brown, one of the most lauded ad agencies in New York City, offered Dean a coveted internship during his senior year at Fordham University. Soon after, Dean was offered a job because of a shining internship, in which his charm and refined nature elicited trust from older colleagues. Sorena could vividly remember the day Dean sat smiling and giddy as if he were a child who peeked at his most anticipated Christmas gifts. He was relentless and bright then. His optimism was contagious, something made easier from landing his dream job that consisted of long lunches with interesting clients and flights to great cities for press conferences and commercials. The accoutrements of dreams, Dean's salary bordered excess, and his Manhattan lifestyle fit the prestige. He was the prototype well-to-do New Yorker, living in a building on the Upper East Side with valet parking and concierge service. He was living the life he talked about as a skinny kid from Queens; a life no one thought possible because during his school years where he was less than motivated. His grades suffered throughout most of high school due to the need to fend off bullies who considered his sexuality a social hindrance. With glazed eyes and bruises beneath the folds of those same eyes Sorena considered beautiful, Dean's voice quivered, "They hate me because I like them…"

Sorena praised the day he came out, and Dean's once dimmed light shone as he began living his truth wholly. No longer harboring the turmoil of being gay and living behind a mask, there arrived assertiveness Sorena—as well as others—found wonderful. A distant wailing from a once shy boy forced to help his struggling family; Dean's family lived by the week; money struggles were apparent. Sorena recalled wondering how Dean's family would help him through college when it was hard to afford a tuxedo for prom. But Dean was scarce throughout his senior year; prom was an afterthought as he went about protecting himself from jocks calling him fag, pole smoker, rump wrangler, and ass prospector.

"Where's Dean?" Sorena's more understanding group of friends would ask.

"Dunno," she'd reply, shrugging. "Hopefully at home studying, he's been kinda hiding out this year, trying to get into college, I guess."

When answering questions from concerned friends, she knew exactly where Dean was. As adults—and saddled with memories of harder times—Sorena would stare across the Williamsburg Bridge toward Manhattan mumbling to herself, "I'm so proud of what you've become."

Sorena was proud that Dean was grinding out a future, taking the A train across the bridge. He was making moves. Those days of his absence were at times draining for her emotional state, but it was decided better to be strong than weak. She had fallen in love with him as years passed. And the love had not dissipated because of his coming out. It was still there, stained and dried against the fabric of her life. She had removed the book he gave her as a Christmas gift from the shelf she came to ignore. And he sat before her, grinning in the present autumn day. In his hand, the usual glass of fine wine aged to magnificence.

"What now?" Sorena asked Dean.

There was silence. Dean had tilted the glass against his lips, the sound of a soft slurp followed. Pulling the glass away he closed his eyes as if entranced.

"The book?" Dean asked.

"I haven't found it yet."

"Maybe he's one of those self-published hermits from New England."

"When did you become an elitist?"

"You're not choosy enough."

"I tried that block of drivel you gave me for Christmas, didn't I?"

"You didn't like it?"

Sorena gave way to a weak smile.

"Anyway, he gave me a letter on the train last week."

"Lemme guess, you haven't read it," Dean mumbled. "Can't believe you didn't like the book I gave you..."

Sorena grinned playfully.

"Okay, I'll read it again. I think I was in a bad mood or something."

"You need a man in your life."

If you only knew, Sorena thought. *And if you only knew I've wanted you…*

"Try'n read every page," Dean said. "I swear you won't regret it."

"Okay, I'll give it another look," Sorena said.

"Besides, it'll be a big help."

"Help for what?"

Dean took another sip of his wine. A hard swallow followed.

"Didn't know any other way to tell you…"

"Tell me…?"

Dean shifted in his seat, his eyes wandering across the bar as though his words and thoughts had exited into the streets of Lower Manhattan.

"Brown's moving me…"

"What?"

"They're transferring me to Chicago."

"Chicago?"

"Yeah, big shoulders, deep dish, miracle mile, the Bears…"

"Not funny, Dean!"

"I know, sorry."

"When were you planning on telling me?"

"Right this minute…"

Sorena made a face, thought of Queens and the subway, long nights consoling Dean and laughing when things transitioned toward happier thoughts.

Sadness came instantly.

"Tell me about the letter from this guy," Dean said.

Sorena shook her head "Right now I just wanna cry," she said. "You were right. I haven't read it yet."

Dean sighed, ran his pointing finger around the rim of his glass.

"Knew it..." Dean began, "You never give adventure much of a chance, do you?"

"It's kinda creepy, don't you think?"

"September 11th, that was creepy! Come on, if you got through that..."

Sorena did not want to talk about 9/11. She remembered how her apartment building shook, and the smell of fire and ash that covered Manhattan for a month. And how the bar in which they were sitting would never be the same again, never feel like a place to make memories and laughter so they could hide the pain of a city scarred.

"Okay, I'll read it," said Sorena. "But not now...you're really leaving?"

"I'm afraid so."

Sorena could not think of anything else. The saying, *'when I leave'* echoed through her apartment in a ghostly fashion. There was now heaviness within her body. She turned away, cleared her throat.

"Don't cry," Dean said. "Love, I'll be fine."

Saying nothing, Sorena could only think, *What about me? What about how I feel about you? What about our time in Queens, and how we would sneak to Manhattan and try to go to concerts at Webster Hall, the Knicks games we loved, the obscure theatrical productions in Brooklyn?*

"Please see me before you go."

"You say that like I wouldn't," Dean replied. "Maybe next week we can have lunch. The rest of this week is bogged down, big clients coming in for a week. But don't worry."

****

The day had come toward its final hours and Sorena still had not read the letter. Distracted by Dean's sudden announcement, concentration failed her. As the sky over the city transitioned to its majestic hues of orange and blue, Sorena decided to read the book Dean had gifted her one year earlier. After a few pages, she began to realize why Dean had given her the book. The clarity of his gesture, so simple, she wished she hadn't been so quick to avoid the words.

This book, she thought, *it's about change…*

Sorena remembered how Dean smiled when handing her the package. It was the same wide grin he gave her before hopping the train for Queens during the summer of 1991. She had not realized Dean was perhaps preparing her for this time in their friendship. His motions were slow, as if he wanted the moment to last. The time had developed in front of her like the gradual development of a black and white photograph. Occurrences simple and common, things like the old woman she did not know who rode the train back to Queens each day, the same old woman she had seen before, the one resembling her grandma. She appeared angry most times—perturbed by her own unadventurous life. The assumption, one typical to old New Yorkers, left Sorena to wonder if the old woman hadn't seen other parts of the world and she had only known the cluttered magnificence of Manhattan.

Often Sorena caught the old woman staring. She once imagined a plausible theory: *Maybe I'm a younger version of her...*

It was sad to think the old woman was once a beautiful and vibrant New Yorker. She was imagined as a frequenter—the Metro A going east toward the city. She was going to the city to meet friends, and a guy named Salvatore, a large Italian man with dark, raven-toned hair and dark skin. His smile was mischievous, crooked. Did she ever marry him? Soon there came the horrible revelation the elderly woman was a snapshot of her life. There before her was her future, unable to be altered by anything physical. Her future was with a man who might bring her sadness. He would be abusive, self-obsessed and live without dreams. His life would remain the same. He would care more for his friends. There would be a life of frightening loneliness.

Thinking of this Sorena remembered smiling in the woman's direction—hoping she would return the gesture. But she had done nothing like this, and there was no revealing of emotions to confirm she was indeed real.

Sorena suddenly found herself away from the book Dean had given her and falling toward her floor were tears. The letter from the man she barely knew sat untouched, aged slightly by the crumpling of its form. Thinking of the old woman and her assumed misery was all she could bear. And thus, she walked toward her bedroom where the letter was placed when she received it.

****

The next day, looking toward her nightstand, Sorena was not shocked by the hour of 11am. It was the weekend, and life was slow, made slower by thoughts of Dean being away from the city she loved had come so soon. "I have to finish this book," she mumbled. In her solemnity, a dream of her past came, and there she was: a student at Lakeshore High in Queens. Prodded by Dean to read an average yarn, she recalled her disdain toward *The Catcher in the Rye* by Salinger. And it was eighteen years later the sound of Salinger's voice still pinched her nerves.

The next day Dean was gone

****

The train arrived at eleven, screeching to a halt louder than usual. With his journal in hand, Baine thought of what he would do to waste the day. The doors opened on the train, and he watched the rush of passengers exit and board. The weekend train was crowded, and he imagined where all of the people were going. *So many people*, Baine thought as he began moving toward the back of the train in search of a space that enveloped solitude.

It was a day of watching people, and there would be a search for someone like him, someone who was successful in the art of writing.

Leaning over his journal, he adjusted his shirt and wrote.

I'm on the train, heading to Manhattan with the rest of the world. I'm a successful author. I'm never alone in the city of many souls. But there's an emptiness I feel. I'm hoping it's because Cyrano is dead. I am on the train he rode the day he came to New York, the C Local it's called. I think he is gone for now. I can't help but stare at the seat he sat in when I first discovered he had followed me all the way here. I wish there was the remnants of his being lying in the emptiness...dust there, dust made of his crushed bones, the crushing of them I crave immensely. I cannot believe I'm here again....

Baine was interrupted by an old man fumbling with an umbrella. He thought of thunderstorms in Alabama.

I cannot believe I love a woman I have no reason to. I haven't seen her on the train since the day I gave her the letter. The memory of her, so much like a dream or the passing of subliminal beauty. I wonder where she is in this busy place. I hope she is still in New York. I hope she is the same woman.

****

Sorena was ready for the day. On her body, the softness of a cotton cardigan the color of pink, one like her mother wore. Along with the sweater that aided in good memories of her mother, she slid upward on her smooth legs jeans she wore scarcely. Her hair was down, dark and shining against the bright color. She applied makeup, more than ever before because she had wanted her face to look different, more alive. Dean had once commented on the amount she applied, so the rebellion was on, thick and necessary. She kept telling herself this was not done out of anger. She loved Dean more than anything, but he was leaving. She thought, *Today I won't think of him, I'll begin moving on...*

On occasion, Sorena would rest her anxious emotions against the thickness of good memories. *I'll deal with it later,* she thought. *For now, I'll fake being happy.*

Grabbing a scarf from her closet, she headed for her front door. Along the hall was where she sat the book Dean had bought so she could read snippets of it throughout the day. It was *The Cornbread Diaries,* a book written by an author she had forgotten about but one she had unknowingly met.

Dr. Stanton had never enjoyed the smell of bookstores; the stale aroma of aged paper and wood had previously eluded him and made him gather memories of slaving away inside libraries as a student. He had not ventured into a bookstore since Christmas of 1999—the year he discovered his wife enjoyed reading graphic novels written by Frank Miller, which caused his intellectual sensibilities' fits.

Nevertheless, he was there to salve his burning disbelief Baine had accomplished to publish a novel during a dissociative fugue, and the book was written and suitable for picky Northeastern readers.

Approaching the front desk, he was greeted with surprising enthusiasm by a girl wearing a nametag shaped like the island of Manhattan. Her name was Michelle. She looked like a girl from these parts, stylish yet not overly dressed as Stanton assumed New Yorkers were. Her hair was long, dark and curly; she had the pale but beautiful skin of an Ashkenazi Jewish woman, thick shapely eyebrows and full lips.

56

"Can I help you?" Michelle asked.

Dr. Stanton, stunned, gave way to a stutter.

"Yeah...Umm, Yes, I'm wondering if you have a book called *The Cornbread Diaries?*"

Michelle flipped her hair over her shoulder, reached for a stack of books piled next to the cash register. The books appeared new.

"Not sure," she said, smiling. "Lemme take these to the back, I'll check."

While she was gone, Dr. Stanton could not help but think of how Michelle looked like a younger version of his wife. Minus the southern accent, she was the spitting image of her. She had that brightness in her face and eyes, a curiosity as though she hadn't learned all of what was needed in life. Her soft eyes, brown and wide, were curious and clear like the eyes of a baby awaiting stimuli. She did not fit the image of a Manhattanite; she was more like the women Stanton had seen on television: those tough, talkative women from Brooklyn.

When she returned her hair was pulled back, tight and glistening. "My manager told me we're out of that book right now," Michelle said.

Stanton felt as though the air had left the room.

"Out of stock?" he asked.

"Apparently it's pretty popular."

"Hmm...Have you read it?"

"No, I'm thinking I should..."

"I know the man that wrote..."

Dr. Stanton wanted to say, *I know the man that wrote that book. He has a serious mental condition. He's wandering around New York. He could possibly think he's someone else. I'm studying him, learning from him. He's my best subject.*

57

He could be a genius.

"That book, he's a…friend of mine."

"Really?"

"But I do need to order a book for my wife. She loves his work."

He was proud of his lie. Outside, he watched New York and its quickness. Overhearing the ominous hum of the subway below the street, he thought of Atlanta's MARTA (Metro Atlanta Rail Transit Authority) and his wife and things he already began missing. It was only a few days and the smell of grits, eggs, tea, and biscuits escaped him. It was replaced by the aromatic air of New York and the smell of ethnic foods he had never in his life tried. It would be a long before he returned to Georgia, a long time until he came face to face with Baine again. He wasn't angry he gave up his chance to take him. The obsession had returned. He could not wait to receive his copy of *The Cornbread Diaries.*

On the phone with his wife, he could hear the sadness in her voice. He wanted to tell himself it was because the Falcons lost. She had become a fan over the years; this came after months of humoring his love of sports. "Not much longer, honey," Dr. Stanton said, lying as a moment of guilt struck him.

"You likin' the city?" she asked, sighing.

"It's okay. Fast, but okay."

"Uh huh."

"Saw my patient the other day."

"So that means you're coming home soon?"

"Well…"

"Oh, no…"

"I'm tryin' something quite different."

58

"You're not gonna be a…"

"You wouldn't believe what he's doing."

There was silence, a passing subway car, the sound of a dog barking.

"Honey?"

"I'm here."

"My patient has somehow been living here."

"How's that possible?"

"My guess is he knows someone."

"You think he has family in New York?"

Dr. Stanton avoided details. He knew his wife did not care. He pulled his phone away from his face, shook his head.

"I had a dream last night you were on a plane and them nasty terrorists hijacked…"

"Stop that!"

"….This 9/11 stuff has me in a bundle."

"I wish you'd stop worryin'."

Stanton thought of other doctors, their careless wives. Most of them cheated. He was lucky his wife still cared even if it was at the expense of his own tireless research.

"I wish you'd just come home, honestly."

"I'm thinking I might have been wrong in my diagnosis of Baine."

"Well, I'm getting tired…."

"Honey, please it won't be much longer."

Silence again, Stanton imagined his wife contemplating divorce. *Maybe I misdiagnosed my marrying you. You ever think of that Mr. Psychology man…?'*

"…I love you. Be careful."

"Love you too, honey. I'll call you tonight when I get back to my room. Get some sleep."

Sadness arrived with the closing of his phone. The hum of the subway beckoned again; He walked toward the tunnel, no longer thinking of Baine but more of his wife.

****

The cab ride was like his first. This time with an old Italian man with tattoos littering his arm. He was short on words. His deep-set eyes remained affixed on Dr. Stanton in the backseat. Stanton did not give him eye contact and avoided feeling ashamed of efforts to remain aloof. Accustomed now to the way of New Yorkers, he assumed this behavior was typical. There was no talking to the concierge at the hotel when he arrived, he simply nodded, gave way to a weak half-grin, the kind he often got from elitist professors at his alma mater.

Once inside his room, the smell of new sheets and towels was comforting. He could no longer think of his wife and her loneliness.

His cell phone rang as soon as he settled in. The name on the phone came up as:

Leo Grumbine.

Oh no, Dr. Stanton thought.

Leo Grumbine was the head of Psychology at the Georgia State Hospital. A man of concise speech and heavy build, Grumbine was an astute psychologist with intimidating credentials.

He's calling for an update, Stanton thought. He opened the phone.

"Dr. Grumbine?"

"Dr. Stanton?"

Please don't…

"Are you still up east?"

"Yes, sir. Still in New York."

"We will need that report by the end of the month."

"No problem, sir, but there seems to be an error involving the patient."

"An error?"

"I don't think Baine suffers from Dissociative Identity Disorder."

"Then what do you surmise is his current condition?"

"Schizophrenia, sir."

****

On the B heading downtown, the first chapter had drawn Sorena inward. Before her was the story of torture, and the damp, sullen confines of the writer's home known as Pipeshop. The night sounded of crickets and cicadas that sailed upon warm air. The details of his home were vivid, sounds and smells and dialects from commoners fell from the page in an elastic imaginary soup. So taken, she had forgotten time, and could not remember the last time she was late when meeting Dean at their favorite café known as Playwrights, an upscale haunt nestled near a densely populated corner adjacent from Webster Hall. A place where careful lurking would happen once upon men and women of great fame. Dean was not a fan of the aura of celebrity; "I couldn't give a shit about celebs…" Sorena recalled Dean saying. And he wasn't shy of looking the part of nonchalant as he approached the table. Sorena could see Dean's casual clothing was as mellow and slightly opinionated as his demeanor. Lying suitably against his frame was the off-white shirt well suited for the early autumn weather. It clung against his svelte build like tightly pulled curtains. The top button, purposely askew, revealed smooth skin Sorena recalled during their summers on Fire Island and the Coney Island boardwalk. A seasoned New Yorker attuned to the world of fashion could automatically name the brand of shirt and its soft fabric, but Sorena did not care nor did she want to see him like this before he left for Chicago.

Dean was stunning.

She turned away and took in the atmosphere around her, hoping Dean would sit down and tell her that he was indeed staying, and the view of New York before her—one she loved and lived with her best friend—would remain the same, untouched and shaped as she remembered before Dean gave her the news.

Her eyes soon caught a glimpse of flashing cameras.

"Wonder who it could be and why anyone cares?" Dean said, sitting down lazily in the chair.

"Thought I was late," said Sorena.

"Perhaps they're taking pictures of you, my love?" Dean said in an English accent. Sorena laughed, rolled her eyes.

"I can't see from here…"

"How're you?"

"How do you think?"

"Oh, sorry."

"I started that book."

Dean sat up in his chair. The air caught his movement, carrying forth his natural scent. Sorena sighed.

"Good, right?" Dean said.

"Thought provoking, I guess." Sorena said.

"You look like you need a thought-provoking drink, sister."

"Chicagoans are so generous."

Dean smiled.

"Gotta look good for the paparazzi."

"The first chapter was weird though, like it was really strange. I felt like I knew the author."

"Maybe he just writes like someone you know."

"No, something different."

"It's cool to have that ability."

"What ability?"

"To make someone feel like they know you when they really don't."

Sorena shook her head. Looking down toward her purse sitting below her chair she could see the spine of the book.

"Well the writer does actually live here in New York," Dean said.

"So many writers live here," said Sorena.

"Most are young and single too," Dean said and almost appeared to want to stand up and sing. He added, "This Adams guy reminds me of Salinger...Actually...Maybe Roth.

Sorena made a disagreeable face, "Okay, get that drink," she said.

Dean pulled his attention away from the street, summoned a waitress. Sorena studied the approaching waitress and her bubbly bright eyes, red hair and fair skin, her smile was wide and rehearsed. *Off-Broadway actor*, Sorena thought.

She looked back at Dean, and he suddenly appeared sad.

"What can I get you today," the waitress asked.

"Bloody Mary," Dean said.

Sorena soon remembered Dean had once told her that his mother drank Bloody Marys and it was the night before he left for Manhattan that he finally had enough nerve to try the drink himself. It had seemed his drink of choice when coming upon a great change in his life.

The waitress, with her appointed smile, turned toward Sorena...

"Just a White Russian," she said.

Dean continued talking while staring across the street.

"I know what you mean though, seriously..."

"...This is our last drink in the city," Sorena said, interrupting.

"Don't do this," Dean said, shifting within his seat. "This doesn't end anything for us, you know?"

Sorena nodded.

"Chicago's just a city," Dean mumbled, playing with a loose string on his shirt. "We're like brother and sister. I'm sorry I had to take this job. Tony told me they really needed my talent in Illinois. Plus, I'll be making..."

"Please," Sorena snapped. "Don't make this about money!"

"You're still mad about what happened in school, aren't you?"

"Just can't believe you're leaving. It's not like you're hopping the train for some rebellious excursion to Greenwich Village."

Dean turned away.

"Isn't this weird to you?" Sorena asked.

"What this?" Dean replied, turning his attention back toward the street. He had suddenly given up removing the stubborn string.

"It's almost the same way we met back in junior high," Sorena said.

"Guess so..."

"Don't act like you don't remember," said Sorena. "We had to do that damn book report on *The Catcher in The Rye*."

"Oh yeah, the sexual overtones, I remember now."

Sorena laughed nervously as the waitress returned and placed the drinks on the table without smiling. Dean's smile faded as the afternoon sun shone within his eyes. "We were such knuckleheads then," Dean began. "Young and trying way too hard to make shit happen. What in the hell were we thinking?"

Maybe we were falling in love, Sorena thought. She wanted to say this aloud.

"Young and stupid, I'd say," said Sorena. "I just feel like now I don't want anything to happen. Especially because you're leaving..."

Her hand had already moved across the table, and her index finger, extended slowly, was gently wrapped around Dean's hand lovingly, and the sun she noticed in Dean's eyes had reflected the welling of tears.

"Well we can make this a long goodbye," Sorena said softly.

"Definitely," Dean said.

Leaving Playwrights Café, Sorena noticed a gang of opportunistic paparazzi as they gathered around a man and a woman walking across the street. Figuring it was the person she failed to notice earlier, she remembered what Dean said once when witnessing celebrity life: "There they go taking pictures of beauty they'd normally never see in their pitiful lives…"

She smiled and could feel the cracking of tears that had dried against the skin of her cheeks.

She knew she would see Dean again.

****

"Something's missing…"

The hush was ominous. His imagination, running wild, had conjured an image of Brooklyn now empty. There was the end of a city awaiting him, and he was the only man alive. His paranoia ran images through his thoughts, snapshots of life before he slept: brownstones; planted trees; the view of a man and woman, faceless and withering and fat, hailing a cab.

If I look outside, he thought, *there will only be dust and rubble…*

He removed himself slowly from his bed, stared at the window. His body had stiffened while resting, and there was a memory of restlessness before he drifted into a pleasant sleep. *Was my restlessness because of nightmares?* he thought.

Then he remembered…

Could it have been Baine summoned a book signing at a bookstore on the corner of Fifth Avenue? To confirm this unusual occurrence there was only one way, and that was to check his journal for previous entries. Cyrano had once unlocked doors in Baine's mind before and had come upon memories and secrets most guarded in the recesses of his thoughts. Done, the dangers were formidable. A subliminal glimpse of his hand moving across pages, the protrusion of a writing utensil in the shape of a female stood erect and gliding across pages made of silk. In block style script, the view of a flier lay in front of him:

BEST-SELLING   AUTHOR   BAINE   ADAMS. AUTHOR OF *THE CORNBREAD DIARIES*...

Damn you, Cyrano!

The opening of his journal stretched dramatically like a dream unfurled. And there before him was something he could not have written nor would he have scribed such untruth. The details were horrid. Baine, peering over toward his bedroom door, hoped he would not hear the summoning of his presence by NYPD.

The journal entry read:

Today's the day! And what a glorious day it is. My first book signing! I can't believe it's finally here! Funny thing, Scribner and Sons' is just across the street from the Barnes and Noble. Their finicky staff rejected many of my manuscripts. Honestly, I hope someone from their company happens to see what is going on this very day. I hope they see that I have something, and my words have caused a further uproar of emotions in a city often full of emotion. It's a day of eye-opening redemption, I must admit.

Baine

There was no hint of his southern likeness in the writing of such a lie. It had to be Cyrano; he was the damn Yankee (something Grandpa called northerners) side of his most wretched behavior.

Soon the memory of what happened came in pieces. Guilt followed. Then fear. Baine discovered Cyrano might have written a book and went about using his name. But what was the title? Who was the publisher? Had anyone else...

Baine started recalling his nightmare, a subtle view in manipulation and his sickness, his encounter with the man in the blue suit. That man he saw outside on the street, the one following him. He was missing. But there was no memory of his name and why he went about searching for him. There were fragments, clues of a life left behind, and a dream followed. Nothing made sense. Cyrano had gained strength and it was time to stop him. The door rattled gently from the intrusion of a gentle breeze. Baine, walking toward the door had begun to smell the aroma of alcohol.

"Cy?" he called out. There was only the greeting of pigeons flying away from the fire escape, wet wings batting against the cool morning air. Again, the smell of drunkenness wafted past his sense of smell. "Cy?" The air back-drafting toward his face gave him the odor of inebriation with strength more foreign than previous. While leaving the sanctity of his bedroom he saw the culprit: an empty bottle of Boone's Farm lay empty, leaning against the edge of his living room sofa as though awaiting Baine's arrival. It had seemed to come alive. The drained and gleaming bottle caught the sun for its momentary life and came upon its own depletion with utter surprise. Baine's imagination could not help but develop the bottle as an entity that came complete with a personality full of ideas carrying detriment. It began talking:

"The sun feels good on my likeness," it said.

Baine, reluctant to answer, rubbed his eyes to dryness.

"Leave my head," Baine mumbled. "Who drank you anyway?"

"Quite thirsty, you and your roommate," the bottle said, and appeared to adjust its stance against the couch.

"Gotta be fuckin' kidding…"

"Ahh…Forget it. Where's the bedroom?"

"It's where I poured you away last week, you fool!"

"No, you actually hid me in another place, remember?"

Baine thought for a moment: Cyrano must have…

"I remember now, I drank you last week before I started writing," Baine said.

"You call yourself a writer?"

"That's what I do!"

"I think Cyrano is the one better with words."

"He's not real."

"You expect me to believe a man that talks to an empty bottle of Boone's? You have any idea how cheap I am?"

"That's it…!"

Baine began approaching the bottle, his hand out and reaching toward the lower end of the sofa.

The bottle rolled away.

It came to a sudden stop against the shoes of a stranger. Looking up in surprise, Baine was greeted by the same man he only knew as the man who followed him on the subway. It was the man in the blue suit. His angular face was cut in two shades by the incoming morning sun.

"Mr. Adams?" the man said calmly while reaching inside his jacket pocket. He revealed then a book with a yellow cover.

Baine read the cover: *THE CORNBREAD DIARIES…*

"Who are you," Baine yelled. "What're you doing inside my house? How'd you…find me?"

"I think you know who I am," the man said.

"Get out and take the fuckin bottle with…!"

"I'm   Dr.   Stanton,   Mr.   Adams."

"Leave, now! Or…"

Baine stared at the bottle lying against Dr. Stanton's feet. It had stopped talking to him. Its simplicity was haunting. He wanted the bottle to continue antagonizing.

"You don't remember me?" Dr. Stanton asked.

"What is this?" Baine asked. "I did nothing; whatever you're here for…Cyrano did it. I swear he did!"

"Cyrano's still here?" Dr. Stanton inquired.

"I was with him last night."

"Where is he, Baine?"

"I dunno."

"I thought he stopped bothering you."

"How do you know him?"

"I met him when you were in Georgia, remember?"

"Georgia?" said Baine, his eyes wide with shock.

"Yes, I'm your…"

Dr. Stanton moved slowly toward Baine. The bottle rolled away from his foot. "Baine," Dr. Stanton began in a soft, sympathetic tone, "I know the family you've created. Do you remember Grandpa, Momma…?

"Momma?" Baine said, stepping backward. "You know my momma? Is she here?"

"Baine your mother left you many years ago."

"No, I…I…saw her…"

"Baine, please. It's time to come back. We need to get you help."

"Momma's here, I know it! She left and came here, and I'm gonna find her."

Dr. Stanton appeared saddened.

"No, Baine. You left. I'm sorry but your mother died when you were young. You don't remember?" Dr. Stanton said.

"Momma's still alive!"

Dr. Stanton showed Baine his copy of *The Cornbread Diaries*. "This is how I found you," he said.

Baine could feel his heart slowing its pace. The room began to melt in front of him. Dr. Stanton melted toward the floor. The last thing he heard was the hushed voice he heard earlier when lying in his bed. It came again. It held the same airy tone and whisper. "Something's missing..."

The room went black.

Remembering Baine during earlier sessions Dr. Stanton could not fathom the changes in his physical structure. No longer was he diminutive and waif. He gathered the maturity of a man of thirty years. His face, although still soft and slight with stubble, gained wrinkles hinting stress and sadness. His forehead creased upon the asking of questions. He recalled a much younger man with scared eyes and shaking hands; a man with matted hair and nervous ticks. There was an aura of calm once foreign.

Dr. Stanton stared, watched his movements before proceeding.

"I remember the last train ride," Baine began. "...Came at eleven in the morning."

Stanton, surprised, asked Baine to repeat his statement.

"Baine, I'm sorry. Can you…?"

"You asked me what my last memory was, right?"

"Oh yes, right…Continue," Stanton replied, lying.

"The train came at eleven, and I was thinking of what I would do that day…"

"What day, Baine?"

"I think it was…"

"It's okay, just tell me why you decided to leave the hospital and come to New York. You know there are a lot of people who miss you back in Georgia."

Baine shook his head as though a bug were crawling on his scalp.

"You know why I came…Momma left, and I wanted to come find her."

"Who again is Momma?"

Baine sat silent. The wrinkles in his forehead deepened.

"Baine?" Dr. Stanton asked.

"You ask dumb questions and I'm gonna just sit here and stare at you like you're some kinda idiot. You Yankee people sho' do ask a lot of dumb questions."

"I'm from the south too, Baine."

"You look like a Yankee, that blue suit and all."

"Actually, I didn't pack enough clothes for my trip."

Baine snickered.

"So…?" Dr. Stanton began.

"I was wondering where all the New York folk go on nice days. It was warm and I was fixin' to ride the subway. You ever ride the metro? Confusin' as hell…"

Dr. Stanton nodded.

"…I was jus' writin' in my journal, takin' notes for my book."

"This book?" asked Dr. Stanton, holding up a copy of the *The Cornbread Diaries*.

"No," Baine said. "Not that one. It was for another…"

Baine stopped speaking. He stared at the book.

"What's wrong, Baine?" Dr. Stanton asked.

Baine shook his head, shrugged.

"Baine?" Stanton said.

"Lemme ask you sumthin'…"

"Sure, go on."

"How'd you and your wife meet?"

"We…"

"Well, I'm gonna just tell you the way you met your wife cannot compare to the way I met a woman on the train."

"What do you mean?"

Moving away from the table, Baine sighed. His face had suddenly become reddened by evident humiliation. Dr. Stanton knew this look. It was the same look he assumed was on his face when speaking of meeting his wife for the first time. It was the look of a man in love. The look of a man unraveled and opened for the world before him; Baine gathered his words carefully.

"Her name…Sorena…"

Dr. Stanton nodded.

"…Ever get that feeling in your stomach—that feeling like if she left the room, she'd take all the air with her? Huh, you ever feel that?'

"Of course, Baine, but…"

"How'd you and your wife meet?"

It was a day Stanton did not want to recall while in New York, while away from his wife. The memory, when it came to him, brought forth an urge to hug her close or kiss her gently on her cheek. Thinking of this and her absence from his life saddened him.

"We met at a store in Decatur," Dr. Stanton said. "She was buying fruit at an open-air market."

Baine smiled.

"I bet you always think of the fruit she was buying, whatever it was. I bet..."

"Apples," Dr. Stanton said, interrupting. "It was apples."

"They never taste the same I take it?"

Baine was right.

They never tasted quite the same after their meeting. It was hot that day, the summer of 1965. He can still catch the smell of her, but only upon the southern air. The aroma of lilac and dove soap failed replication in the northern regions.

Dr. Stanton switched the subject.

"Tell me more about this Sorena," Dr. Stanton said.

"Cyrano wants her."

"What?"

Baine moved back toward the table, leaned forward. "If I talk about her, Cyrano will come in here and bother me. He followed me here to New York. I asked him for help..."

"Help with what?"

Taking a deep breath, Baine sat back in his chair.

"You may not know this, but there's sumthin' about beautiful women I find..."

"Intimidating?"

"No, much deeper than..."

"Oh, they scare you?"

Baine nodded.

"Like a rabid raccoon in the night, doctor. This woman scares me. Its why Cy came and started screwing my life up again."

74

Dr. Stanton could not document fast enough. Awaiting Baine's switch toward the persona of Cyrano, he hoped his hasty summation of Schizophrenia was correct. Baine was peering behind Dr. Stanton, waiting for Cyrano's arrival. Dr. Stanton wrote in clear legible print: I WAS WRONG ALL THE TIME, CLEARLY AN EGREGIOUS ERROR. I'VE FAILED...

"Is Cyrano here now?" Dr. Stanton asked.

Baine nodded, pointed toward the door.

"What's he doing right now?"

"The same thing I'm doin', doc. He's waitin' on the rest of the story about you and your wife. How you two met and all..."

Leaving the room, Dr. Stanton realized he did not want to reveal the specifics of how he met his wife. He thought he could feel Cyrano's body pressed against his, subtly urging him to speak and give in to Baine's request.

He was on the phone in his hotel room.

"Hello," Stanton said.

There was dead air.

"Hello?" his wife suddenly responded.

"Oh, you're there."

"Where would I go?"

He thought of the fruit store, how she looked that day, her scent, and the summer heat.

"I'm sure you haven't stayed inside all this time," Stanton said.

She sighed, said, "It's been raining too much here. Not in the mood to drive. How are you, honey? You sound tired."

"Just got in from interviewing my patient..."

"How'd it go?"

Dr. Stanton could not find the words to respond; words confessing his failure. He looked at the wall in front of him, imagined the words scribed within the paint and constructed them.

"There have been some new developments," he said. "It's all I can say. But I'll be back by the end of the week."

No answer from his wife. Stanton heard subtle sounds of thunder in the background.

"Hello?"

"It's really rumbling," his wife said. "You hear that?"

"Yes...Yes...I heard it. Maybe you should stay in."

"Well, you get some rest and call me tomorrow. Let me know when you're leaving. I miss you."

"Miss you too."

Opening her mailbox, a surprise greeted Sorena. It was the view of one letter. She reached inside, pinching it between her fingers. The envelope was thick and smelled like burnt coffee and wood. It reminded her of old bookstores in Greenwich Village, which induced a smile she thought would fail to arrive again. She thought about how Dean sent her letters when on business trips, the letter he sent when he first arrived in Manhattan. The words, scattered and quite random, highlighted his excitement and the disorganization of his new freedom. His penmanship took the place of his being there, long letters pressed hard into the paper like ditches in earth, ink smudges revealed he was either sweating profusely or crying due to missing Sorena. Dean was always writing letters from bookstores where he scrounged for new literature or from coffee shops where he'd seek men of his liking, men he thought he'd marry. From there he would shove the letter into jeans tight enough to appear as though they were painted on his legs. The paper consumed perspiration from his skin while he moved throughout New York. The thoughts, words, and feelings gathered upon the paper he wrote on like dust to moistened wood.

Although comforted by thoughts of Dean's letters, Sorena was soon affixed in the reality that the handwriting on the front of the envelope was not from the man she knew and loved. There was no return address. It was now a strange thing, a parcel from an unknown company or a person she could not conjure or fathom as anyone she knew.

Then she remembered.

"…That man from the train?" she whispered.

The B going toward Queens, the writer; his name was Baine and the image of him developed in front of Sorena. The way he smiled, a wry grin full of bashfulness like that of a boy caught in the act of lustful longing. He was from Alabama, had written a book. His accent was thick. His hair cut short and lined up around the edges in a manner precise and clean. He was handsome, a nice man with a dream that seemed to bulge from his personality as though he had been eating it all his life.

"My goodness," she mumbled. "It's the book…*The Cornbread Diaries.*"

****

Waiting for the subway, the sound of the incoming train screamed against Sorena's memory of Baine. Upon the arrival of the B heading toward the Village, she could not quite remember him as she wanted. In pieces she developed him, first by scent, the subtleties of hotel room soap or something not quite as expensive in comparison to the overpriced soap Dean used. The naps of hair combed hard and matted from relentless patting to form a suitable shape. His smile was genuine, not quite pained like older black men of York City, not like the ones from Brooklyn who hated coming to Manhattan. Void was the look on Baine's face as though he would never in his life return home the same. Baine revealed a man whose clothes fit well, were void of bagginess, and his pants were too high for the cut of his shoes—the color of brown and not a brand she was familiar with. His shoes leaned toward the side from constant wear, the soles, uneven, appeared melted from the friction of walking. His demeanor was slow and thoughtful. He was southern with niceties Sorena found disarming. But on his wrist was something she could not understand. A band, as though he was recently released from the hospital, a band the color of baby blue.

She was soon skimming the pages of *The Cornbread Diaries*, hoping she could hear his tone, imagine the movement of his lips and the cadence of his slow speech. His voice was thick and smooth like hardened molasses, his demeanor the same, sweet and sticky.

Hoping to rediscover his charm, Sorena happened upon a smile that didn't feel forced. Dean had yet to call her and his eventual relocation brought on an emotional burden she wanted to escape, so she reveled in the comforting admiration of another. Resting upon her tense shoulders were the memories of travels and nightly gatherings at the café, memories that now poked and prodded her skin causing her skin to itch from anxiety. Sorena, scolding herself internally, she had never longed for the mere presence of a man. As a child, her father, a cold, hard-working man could not conjure such longing and seemed jealous of her close friendship with Dean. "What's the deal with you and this

Dean kid," he'd ask, standing within the doorway of Sorena's bedroom with his arms crossed. Sorena later wished it was her father giving in to the protective traits she longed for, but he never asked again and instead gave way to eye rolls and heavy sighs. Numerous boyfriends and potential mates were tested, some lasted and others were too fearful. *"I like you, but…"* became the words uttered by many men in her life.

Dean was a vessel for her impending fate toward true love—the man that flew away on the air of life's wistful mysteries

In one sharp motion, Sorena turned her head away from the rear door, reapplying the mental armor within. *Why on earth am I looking for a man I only met once*, she thought. The writer from Alabama would not appear. He would not come and distract her from the shifting in her life.

****

Dr. Stanton wanted the room to feel cold. Warmth would cause distraction. He had learned during his brief introduction of Cyrano the "writing thing" was a figment developed from elements of New York, and he was not fond of southern heat. Months before Baine vanished, he discovered this through an argument, one of which came during a session. Astounded, Dr. Stanton could not take notes due to his hands shaking from excitement. Later he recorded the occurrence on his hand-held tape recorder. "A major breakthrough today," he began. "Cyrano comes by changes in temperature."

The room was fifty degrees. The air outside danced with warmth and the music was early autumn. Mild, a degree of sixty.

Cyrano would arrive to be studied.

The subtle whirr of air conditioning was all that could be heard. New York sounds mixed with the hum. Dr. Stanton, looking up toward the clock on his wall, waited. It was noon. He surmised the sun would bring Cyrano. "Bet you think Cy is here," Baine said. He was slouched in his chair, manipulating a hangnail on his left index finger. It broke away fell toward the floor. He looked sad.

"Well," Dr. Stanton began. "Is he?"

Baine shrugged.

"Dunno, doc." Baine said. "You tell me."

"We should start with you telling me about the book."

Baine made a face; started tugging on another finger.

"What book, the one Cy wrote?"

Stanton nodded.

Baine sat up in his chair, adjusting his shoulders as if something bothersome had perched on them.

"I gave him an idea before I left Alabama," Baine said. "He kinda ran off with it. A small story about some kid from the south who wants to be a writer and live in New York City; I told him not take my idea…" Baine paused. Looking over his shoulder, he stared out of the window. "…You ever hear so many horns in your life?"

"No Baine, well, maybe sometimes when I'm driving downtown in Atlanta. You remember Atlanta, right?"

Baine sighed. "Oh, that place," he breathed.

"You do remember?"

"I know I don't like the south much. People talk funny and move too slow."

"Sounds like something Cy would say."

"He did actually say that. I remember one time when drunk he started a fight at this bar in the Village. Funny thing, it was with two girls. One was from San Francisco and the other was from somewhere in Michigan. He told them they were not real New Yorkers until after the ten-year mark."

"I've heard that myself."

"Shrinks hear everything; bet you could hear a fly fart if you listened hard enough."

Dr. Stanton smiled, stifled a laugh.

"So, has Cyrano come to our session?" Dr. Stanton asked.

Baine's shoulders slumped.

"He's standing at the door," Baine said. He did not bother to turn and look.

"That door?" Dr. Stanton asked, jerking his thumb toward the direction.

"Yeah."

"So why doesn't he come in?"

"It's too warm."

****

Lured by the fifth chapter, Sorena could not remove her eyes from the page. Each word was tangible and had become the necessary replacement regarding Dean. The scenery of a town mentioned in *The Cornbread Diaries*, a town known as Pipeshop, replaced Manhattan. Tall, weeping willow trees shaded her warmth and caressed her body more than the whistling heat from the radiator in her apartment. She could see the character known as Grandpa as he sat on the porch shirtless while sipping a tall glass of homemade lemonade. She could taste the lemon drops, and see the little girl mentioned by the main character, a girl who captured his interest. Passion was abounding in the letters he composed for the little girl. Her hair, described as smelling of sweet, raw honey matched evenly with skin the color of caramel and eyes brown that shone like Milk Duds; her lips were red like cherry-flavored licorice. He wrote about his love for her and described in detail the sagging willow tree branches that hung over his head and how they inspired. He wrote:

I think of you during the most subtle, tranquil moments of life…

Her name was Sarah.

Sorena could not imagine having a man long for her in such a way. She had dated many men; none of whom were passionate. The lines she recalled hearing from suitors became testaments of her love life:

"It's not you, it's me."

"I need space."

"Can we be friends?"

"I'm not who you think I am…"

She was told beauty was enough. The lie, she was used to hearing. During her younger days, this lesson was not learned. She now knew the barometer of a good man.

When Sorena finally decided to return to the life before her, it was already 9pm. She hadn't eaten dinner. Time dissolved amongst the New York skyline, leaving behind the glow of buildings across the sky. She wondered where Baine was, thought about the subway and his ventures in a city unfamiliar to him. And soon her phone rang, breaking the dream and her star-eyed staring.

83

It was a voice unrecognizable to her ears.

"Hello?"

"My goodness, you're home?"

It was Dean. Sorena sighed.

"You're calling me?"

"I told you, love, nothing's gonna change."

"So, you like the Midwest?"

"It's different."

"How's that?"

"Not a lot of gay men."

"See, told you not to leave."

Dean laughed. Sorena pulled the phone away from her ear, not wanting to hear something she missed so dearly. "Gotta tell you this book is striking a chord," Sorena said.

"Got to the fifth chapter, I see," Dean replied.

"Yeah, how'd you know?"

"I *know* you."

"Seems like this guy is writing a love letter to all of the women he's ever came in contact with."

"Well, it's my letter to you."

"Ahh, you're such a girl."

"Only in my dreams, love."

Sorena laughed. It was the hardest laugh she'd had since Dean left.

"So, what is the call for?" Sorena asked.

"Looks like I'll be back in New York for a conference in a few weeks, wondering if you'd like—"

"Duh, now you're clueless and gay."

"Stop it!"

"Stupid question. Of course I'd like to meet you for one of our famous Greenwich Village drinking sessions."

84

"Nice."

"Can't wait to see you."

"Hold that thought."

"Holding."

"See you soon, love."

****

Written on the wall inside Baine's room were words written by what Dr. Stanton knew as the "writing thing" from the south. The temperature was cool and sitting beside Baine's bed on a sparsely occupied table was a small glass filled with store-bought iced tea. The room smelled like mint and sweat. There was a thickness in the air as though moist air had flowed inward from outside.

Cyrano had arrived.

Baine soon turned over, stretched. Dr. Stanton could hear Baine's bones crack. Yawning, Baine mumbled, "They gon' be mad when they see you wrote on the wall."

"Baine?" Dr. Stanton said.

Baine sat up on the bed, rubbed his eyes.

"You were saying something, doc?" Baine said.

"I think it was you who said something about the writing on this wall."

Baine stared at the wall as if it began talking. He grinned.

"Cy, you rascal, how could you?"

"Baine, there's only you and me in this room...You do know that, right?"

Baine turned away from the wall, shook his head.

"Cy's standing right behind you, doc; he doesn't look thrilled ya in this room talk'n to me like he ain't even here. I think ya itchin' to get scratched if you get my drift."

"Why do you feel this man you call the writing thing exists?"

Baine—in a swift motion—stood up from the bed; Dr. Stanton had never experienced violence from one of his patients. Baine appeared taller than he remembered, and he could see his hands curled into a tight, knuckle-whitening fist.

Dr. Stanton recoiled.

"Cy, tell this man why you wrote on this wall," Baine whispered while looking directly behind Dr. Stanton.

He did not bother turning to look.

"You asked how my wife and I met, Baine?"

Baine relaxed his posture, unfurled his fist.

"Oh, you never did tell me. How'd you meet her, first describe her so I can get a picture…I like being able to see a person."

Dr. Stanton remembered her as a young woman; now seeming as though a fantasy, recalling her youth contrasted heavily against the marks of aging. Her lips had thinned, and her skin appeared cracked and dried in places, there was a lack of body to her hair, and her teeth had darkened from her smoking habit. But he still loved her. And he hadn't wanted to remember her as the young girl he met at the farmers market many years ago.

"Why such interest in how I met my wife?" Dr. Stanton asked.

Baine sat down on the bed.

"I just wanna know if this woman I met on the train is a woman I'm in love with."

"There's no way to know that unless…"

"Unless what?"

"Unless you spend time getting to know her."

"Why're people so big on that? Don't you just know in that instance? Cy helped me write many a letter to her and those words were sure about love and they felt like it too. Hours, I spent hours, makin' sure I picked the right words, and when he wrote them…I could feel it."

Dr. Stanton was saddened by the look in Baine's eyes. A longing he hadn't seen since Bogart in *Casablanca* or the look of one of his patient's spouse after she committed suicide.

"It takes time to know someone and love them, Baine," Dr. Stanton said. "And I'm sure you wrote those letters yourself as well as that book."

"I didn't."

Baine removed himself from the bed again. Walking over toward the wall, he spat on the palm of his hand and began erasing the writing.

"Sorry, Cy," Baine began. "Doc is difficult today."

"I'm not difficult, Baine. There's no one here but us."

"He's givin' you such a funny look right now."

"That's just it, Baine. It's only you that sees this man."

"You better stop playin' with me like that."

"This is not a game."

"Then why's Cy laughing at you?"

"It's you that finds this humorous."

Baine halted his scrubbing on the wall. He looked over toward the door. "Momma's going to come visit me in this place too if she can find her way through New York," Baine said, smiling as though someone tickled him.

Dr. Stanton stifled a sigh.

"She never existed," Dr. Stanton said.

"How'd I know you'd say that?"

"Guess we've been doing this for a long time."

No longer did he want to talk about his wife. Soon he would see her again, and the thought of remembering when she was young and energized by the electricity that was southern life in Atlanta caused him not to bear thinking of her home and confined by domesticity. He imagined her waiting on the couch in their living room, the warm southern breeze thick with the smell of peach trees entering through the screen door from the rear of the house, blowing her graying locks with subtle and caressing gusts. She'd occupy her time by crocheting habit while there sat a glass of wine on the living room table atop a coaster bathed in the temperature of the room; the lit cigarette she swore never to smoke now lit due to her nagging nerves and missing the only man she ever loved.

On the phone, he could hear the wind he thought of just moments before.

"Raining hard here," his wife said.

"I think it's coming this way."

"Well, as long as the weather is nice when you fly home."

"Still shook on flying, may just take the train again. Should be soon, I think I'm making progress with my patient."

"That's good. Not sure if I want you to fly either."

"Are you smoking again? Your voice…"

"No, I'm actually in the sunroom watching the storm."

"I miss thunderstorms."

"Huh?"

"I said I miss thunderstorms."

"Oh."

He wanted her to agree.

"Remember when we used to sit and watch them together?"

"It's the reason I'm doing it now?"

Dr. Stanton sighed.

"Well, you get some rest tonight. I'll see you soon. Love you."

"Love you too."

"Goodnight."

"Night, sweetie."

The call disconnected, and he wished he was there.

****

Sorena felt like it was high school again. Waiting for Dean to come upward on the escalator at LaGuardia, she was that girl with big hair and a penchant for punk rock and bands whose names she could not pronounce. As arrivals came and went and hugs were exchanged with smiles and tears, she thought of Dean's email, and how she could not concentrate after reading it.

Hey, love. I'm coming back to the apple this weekend. Sorry, short notice, but it's me, and that is how I do things as if you haven't noticed. Oh, something I forgot to mention: I met someone here in Chinatown, I'll save you the details. Gotta go catch a bird.
LOVE…

His smile was as she remembered. It had the same brightness and came with the same ease. He had not quite left the New York they shared, but there was easiness about his nature Sorena had never witnessed before.

"LaGuardia," Dean began. "Still the relevant nightmare this time of year."

Sorena took in his scent as she always did. It was spicy and dense. They embraced like lovers.

"So good to see you," Sorena said, smiling, feeling as though her cheekbones would push through her face.

"Let's get out of here," Dean said. "Before I get arrested for indecent behavior," he added.

They left the airport holding hands.

****

That night Dean undressed in her living room like when they were young. His body—physically void of prime adult years—failed to look as Sorena once remembered. No longer was there thickness around his waist, and his rib cage gave hints toward subtle protrusion. His arms lacked tone. "You need a good Italian meal from Toni's," Sorena said.

Dean smiled, revealing straight white teeth that had not changed in the slightest.

"Oh, love," he began, "just not eating right; they have me doing a lot out there. I'm up all night and just don't have the free time I had when I was here."

Dean said this while sliding out of his pants like a shedding reptile.

"So, tell me about this guy," Sorena said.

Dean blushed.

"He's tall," Dean began, "educated, looks good in a Versace shirt. Got any wine in this place?"

Sorena laughed. "That's a dumb question," she said. "You forget who you're dealing with, mister. Besides I haven't drank since you left, just didn't seem the same."

Sorena walked toward her kitchen while taking in Dean's smile and hoped he wouldn't look as thin when she returned.

"You need to tell me about the book," Dean said. "Did you ever get to meet the author and tell him about your crush?"

"Admiring someone's work does not mean you have a crush on them. Besides I'm too old for crushes." Sorena heard Dean giggle like a child while pouring a glass of Pinot Noir.

"This guy I met seems nice. I'm not too sure about him though," Dean said. Walking back toward her living room, Sorena marveled at how Dean scrunched his body on her couch. *Could he do that before?* she thought.

"Not sure about him?" Sorena asked.

"He's your typical playboy," said Dean.

"And you're not?" Sorena asked facetiously.

Dean gave way to his new giggle. Sorena handed him his glass and watched as he sipped.

"No longer doing that, love. I'm too old and my cock isn't as thick."

"You're so eloquent."

"You're so in love with me."

He's right. Damn him, Sorena thought.

"Well, I haven't seen that writer since you left."

"Good book though, right?"

"Damn good."

"You should call the publisher, get a hold of his agent, get lunch with him."

"Yeah, right, okay."

Dean's face indicated he was not joking.

"You're serious?" Sorena asked.

"As serious as when I came out on the subway. Remember that?"

"Don't remind me."

****

That day, on the C Local platform, Dean attempted telling Sorena his life-changing revelation. Sorena could only tell it was something friendship-altering by the look in his eyes. The guilt she felt for not clearly affirming his feelings toward men came as dreams of the moment.

Keep away from the closing doors, please…

"Did you hear what I said," Dean asked.

"Yeah, yeah I heard. Dean…"

"You didn't say anything."

"I couldn't hear you."

"I'm gay, Sorena."

Next stop, Hoyt-Schermehorn….

"Shit," Sorena would say.

"What?"

"We got on the wrong, fuckin' train…"

****

The receptionist's voice was youthful. "Marchen and Stark Publishing," she said giddily. Sorena waited long enough for her to repeat the name.

"Marchen and…"

"Uh, yes, I'm a journalist for a local East Village publication," Sorena began, lying. "We'd like to interview one of your authors."

There was a pause.

"Okay, which…?"

"…The author of *The Cornbread Diaries*."

"Oh. Hold on, I'll get you to the right person."

There was no hold song while she waited. There was only the sound of rustling papers. Then, the sound of a muffled voice came.

"Interview?" the voice said.

Someone picked up the phone.

"Hello?"

It was the voice of a man.

"Yes," Sorena said. "I'm calling to see if there's any way possible I could speak to an author by the name of Baine Adams? He wrote *The Cornbread Diaries*?"

There was a long, uncomfortable pause.

"Baine?" the man said.

"Yes, Baine Adams. I'm with Village Weekly…"

"Village Weekly?"

"Yes, we're new."

"I guess if the Village Voice frowns on our authors we'd be glad to have you interview one."

"Can you get me in contact with…?"

"You do realize we're a vanity house, right?"

Sorena looked at her bookshelf and thought of her arrogance and snobbery. She had never bought a novel written by an author published through a vanity press.

"I do," Sorena said.

"Give me one minute."

The silence on the phone was irritating. Sorena imagined the three people in the office staring at the phone while they steadily devised a plan to sound legitimate.

"Excuse me, your name?" the man asked. Sorena gave a pseudonym and smiled like she did when she was fifteen years old and lied to her mother.

The man on the phone sighed.

"You're not with that hospital, are you?" he asked.

"Hospital?" Sorena replied.

"Yes, from what I know he had some shrink. A psychologist looking for him about a week ago. We thought it was odd but didn't think much of it. After September 11th, things like that seem trivial, you know?"

"I understand."

"Yeah, sorry."

"It's okay. Did they happen to tell you why they were looking for him?"

"Confidentiality, they couldn't say too much? We didn't ask. Look, ma'am, we work out of a small shop in Brooklyn. This guy calling himself Baine sent us his manuscript about a year ago and we thought it was pretty cool, But then, September 11th...we had to wait to publish it."

"Oh, yes. It's actually really good," Sorena said. She had now forgotten her lie.

"Best way to get a hold of him now is to check hospitals in the area."

Hospitals? Sorena thought. *He seemed so...*

"Well, thank you. Sorry to bother you."

Sorena hung up.

The look on Dean's face that evening frightened her. With his unexplained weight loss, his frown was deep and made his face take on the shape of a man nearing middle age.

"Meet all kinda weirdos in New York," Dean began. "The creative ones are the worst."

Sorena stared at the cover of *The Cornbread Diaries*.

"There's something weird about this whole thing. He seemed so…"

"Still naïve."

"Whatever."

"The best ones, love. All of them…C-R-A-Z—"

"S-T-O-P!"

"Drinking that cheap Pinot has your 'crazy' radar all coo-coo."

"This Pinot is about as old as your ability to be sarcastic."

"The flavor does not reveal its true essence through age."

"What you need is some pasta. Toni's?"

"Not up for food."

"Goodness. How're you surviving Chicago? The food there…"

"Just haven't been hungry lately."

Dean's grim face attempted to lift.

"Everything okay?"

Dean sipped his wine, placed his glass on the table, and faded away under the soft light glowing from Sorena's lamp. Walking toward the hallway he turned and smiled a drunken smile while stumbling toward the bathroom.

That evening they laughed at their latest ventures. Dean spoke more of his new love interest. His eyes revealed comfort and serenity. "This man…" Dean said, wistfully. Sorena—lost in a moment of memories—momentarily focused on the difference in Dean's appearance, ever so slightly mentally scolding her inebriated state in its failure to cloud thoughts of Dean's frailness. "You're staring awfully hard," Dean said.

"It's dark, can't see…" Sorena replied.

"Liar."

"I'm still bad at lying?"

"You're terrible!"

There came a long silence, the studying of their surroundings. Before Sorena could take another sip of her wine, her comfort with Dean and her often impulsive inquisitiveness beckoned.

"Why're you so thin?" Sorena asked.

Dean frowned while taking his glass to his lips.

"I'm feeling kinda…" Dean began forming his thumb and pointer finger in a shrinking gesture.

"Kinda what?" Sorena said. "I'm just worried you're not taking care of yourself and you're thinking about hopping a train to escape whatever it is you're dealing with and then I won't see you again for months…"

"…Small I guess; like I was moved to Chicago to start something and then get the boot."

"That's not true, Dean." Sorena began. "You have a lot of stake in that company." Dean took a quick survey of his person, poked at his stomach.

"Plus, just lonely," Dean said. "I guess I'm getting depressed and want to stop looking for new adventures. It's getting old. It's like since I left school that day and came to Manhattan, I've been running. I need to settle down."

Sorena sighed. She no longer felt the warmth of her wine-induced buzz. "That'd be strange but it's possible," she slurred.

"I think you need to do the same," said Dean.

"I've tried, and as you can see my luck hasn't changed much."

"So how crazy could he possibly be?"

"Not sure and now I don't think he's the author of that book you gave me. Such a shame…"

"So talented," Dean said, interrupting.

"So, now what?"

"Sounds like we need more wine."

****

There he was, smiling. His hands, on his hips, appeared to dig in his side as though he were searching for the right words through his skin.

"That doctor rubs me wrong," Cyrano said. "I say we make like wind and blow this joint."

"I can't, Cy."

"Why not?"

"Momma's comin' and we gon get thangs right and go home to see Grandpa."

"Still lookin' for that woman that left you at that place? So sad."

"I say you skedaddle your sorry tail back wherever it is you came from. You know you made a fool of me not talkin' to the doc?"

97

"That's only because he had you figured out and I wanted to bask in the comedy."

Baine's middle finger was already exposed, a snarl of contempt on his face. He reached over and turned out the lights. Cyrano stood over him, grimacing.

"Let's get outta here!" Cyrano said.

"What about Momma?"

"If we leave, we can get back to our place and get the money we need to go and find her away from these walls. How's about…"

"You're crazy!"

"That makes two of us."

****

The marble floor hallway in the apartment building appeared cold. In the distance, the glow of an exit sign beckoned. The floor in the hallway shone like latex and the smell of ammonia and bleach came through the door like a scented entity. Baine wanted to smell Sorena. She had become a distant thought, a dream, something that escaped his mind and then would come back strong and tangible as ever. *I should have told her how beautiful she was on the train that day*, Baine thought as he walked back inside his apartment. Looking over toward his bed he could see Cyrano scribbling his plan on a small note card. His eyes scanned the scribbled writing under soft light; he looked hungry and determined, as though the words were cooking, simmering.

Cyrano mumbled, "Should work, yes, this oughta do…"

Baine cringed.

He could see Cyrano pacing the room. He had done this before, inside the apartment, the pacing and biting of his lower lip. His scent from sweating had grown stronger. The smell, like rotting drywall, wafted from his pale exterior like warm bread. He stopped, stared at the wall...

"You know they have cameras in this place, right?"

Baine covered his ears.

"You always know how to crap on an idea, Cy."

"I'm just looking out."

"Glad I stopped those meds."

"So that means you're glad I'm back."

Baine shrugged. He hated when Cyrano was right.

They had done this before. The last time was minimal. The summer of 1985, and the catalyst was the longing of another girl. Her name was Conchetta Violet, and she was the brownest and most beautiful of southern girls. Her eyes always appeared welled and near emission of tears. She was bow-legged and had knees ashy and scabbed from frolic with neighborhood boys and girls much older than her. When she spoke, her words ran together as if painted inside her mind. She was far from perfect but close to everything Baine wanted. And now inside of his apartment in New York City, he could see her waiting in the hallway for him; her hair being twirled by her fingers, and that bowed stance with the knocking of young, scarred knees.

"You think we can get outta here and get your girl?" Cyrano asked.

Baine did not answer. Conchetta gave him a scolding glare. He turned away from the view of her in the hallway, rubbed his eyes.

"Gotta find Momma and..."

There was the interruption of thoughts by intrusive light. Squinting, Baine saw the night security guard walking toward Conchetta, and he waved to her with a sadness he had not felt since Momma left. The guard glanced at Baine, a look of curiosity on his face. Baine turned. Upon looking back, Baine noticed Conchetta vanished and so did the memory of her. It was replaced by the need to escape and find Sorena.

There was an empty room. Dr. Stanton glared at his watch while wondering what time his superior would contact him to relieve him of patient1022. *How could this have happened again?* Stanton thought.

The last time the room was much warmer and the call of wildlife outside was heard in the distance. The cooing of birds and the buzz of cicadas was now replaced by honking horns and the sound of construction equipment. A cab driving by honked its horn. Walking over toward the window Dr. Stanton could not see signs of an escape. The window was high, too high for Baine to climb through. The cab honked again. This time the ominous sound lingered. The cab driver's impatient horn drowned out the sound of a drill. A pigeon flew from the window and Dr. Stanton watched as it flew downward and away from the building he had come to loathe.

He looked at his watch again, sighed.

In walked the night nurse. Her smile was of the humoring kind.

Stanton hated her instantly.

"Are you sure you didn't hear anything?" Dr. Stanton asked.

"I'm pretty sure," the nurse replied.

"Hmm."

"It was pretty quiet last night, Dr. Stanton. It's usually rather calm in here."

"Yeah, I know. It's just that he has a history."

"I know. I'm sorry I…"

"The cameras!" Stanton blurted.

The Nurse flinched.

"Huh?"

"Would we be able to…?"

"Oh right, sure."

"You know where they are?"

"Follow me."

She hovered behind him with a pen twirling through her fingers. Dr. Stanton was tempted to ask for privacy. But his tongue was bitter, and the request would have sounded harsh. There was a simmering anger within him he had not felt since his wife once revealed she was attracted to another man. More than ten years ago this occurred, and each time he grew angry when the comparisons started.

This feels like that time she told me about Gary, that bastard!

There was something about the nurse. She was a younger version of his wife, a girl who appeared to long for the aura of big city living but could not quite find the passion to express it. Her hair was pulled tight, a ponytail straight and thick grazed the small of her back. The mane was blond, near white, platinum, and her eyes were pale-blue and caught the morning sun coming in from outside. She was beautiful and ghostly, attractive and mysterious like all the nurses who worked in mental hospitals. She was not overweight, and she did not smell like chlorinated bleach.

She pointed at the monitor.

"Fuzzy," she began. "But I do see someone."

Dr. Stanton peered closer.

"That's the janitor, right?"

"No."

"Huh?"

"That's not Rodrigo. He walks with a limp."

"Maybe he was off."

"Rodrigo practically lives here."

"Then who is it?"

"Rodrigo's the only night janitor we have."

"Oh, no."

Baine felt out of place amongst the revelers on the subway. The look of a maintenance man was not becoming. He received stares. Horribly, he began thinking that his escape from the mental institution was something being broadcast across all of Manhattan.

Cyrano began laughing.

"This was your idea," Baine mumbled. A woman looked at him, turned away.

"You better stop talking to me; people may think you've just escaped from an insane asylum."

"Not funny!"

"Shh."

I must get off this train, Baine thought.

Cyrano shook his head.

Baine got off at 42nd. The air had become cool, too cool for spring and it made him want his apartment. He wanted to lay on his bed with those disheveled clothes curled against his body, and with a drink—of the alcohol persuasion—on his nightstand. He would sip slowly the warming liquid and think of Sorena. He wondered what she had done without the letters, and if her life had moved on toward new things and, moreover, a new man. He imagined this man: A New Yorker, seasoned and cultured and intelligent and able to carefully analyze letters; a man of broad interest; a man well-traveled and physically striking. He was like the men Baine wrote about in his books. The man he wanted to become.

"Do you think she'll still want to meet me?" Baine asked. He was looking up toward the sky above Manhattan. He longed to see stars and thought of Bessemer during summer.

Cyrano shrugged. "I'm sure it's not you she wants to see," he said, callously.

Baine ignored him.

"Why must you always piss on my dreams?"

"Maybe you really have to take a leak. Wanna piss on mine?"

"You're still a child wearing men's clothing."

Cyrano grinned. Baine was stuck by the browning of his front row of teeth. But this was something he had seen before, the discovery of decay before he left the hospital in Georgia. Nonetheless, it was a mystery due to moments when Cyrano would appear healthy, strong, and clean.

"You been drinkin'?" Baine asked.

"Who, me?"

"No one else is around, Cy."

"How dare you ask, you should know."

Cyrano was right. The night cool suddenly turned toward an uncomfortable chill, and the buildings flanking the sparse surrounding of trees appeared more imposing than ever.

Baine picked up his pace in hopes Cyrano would not be able to keep up. If he thought about it hard enough, he could lose him. There was that corner of his mind where things went to fester: dark places filled with the thick soot of past regrets. There, where all those memories in regard to Grandpa and Momma remained, where the oily and caked residue of fights Baine allowed to happen, binge drinking sessions he could not control and tongue-lashings that made him twitch in his sleep. Momma had a mouth that spewed fire and Grandpa had fists that could crush rocks into powder.

I'd love for Cyrano to go there and never come back, he thought.

He turned around, looked upon the cold that caressed his eyes, and saw nothing but the passing of a cab on a nearby street. Turning back, he looked up toward the sky again. There was a lone twinkle of a star.

He thought it called to him.

Beside Baine's bed in his room there sat a cup full of medication. Dr. Stanton saw a glimpse of his termination and how it would change his life. The view contained a form of the partial disintegration of Chlorpromazine. The sour odor of dried saliva and natural dyes caused him to wince. *He's doing it again*, Stanton thought.

There was the recalling of Baine nearing a stupor when he first started taking the medication.

A MORE MODERATE DOSE MAY BE REQUIRED…

Dr. Stanton had written this on the upper left-hand corner of his notepad. Baine sat still, his head hanging downward toward the floor as if weighted. He was drifting into sleep; a sad sight, the lowering of Baine's dose was sure to relieve the blurred vision, constipation, and dry mouth.

"These pills…" Baine said.

"Yes?" Dr. Stanton replied.

"I can't seem to…"

Baine's shoulder slumped as if the air had left his body.

"…keep food down or stay awake."

A DEFINITE MODERATION IN DOSE. PATIENT APPEARS INCOHERENT AND LETHARGIC.

"I'll see what I can do about lowering the dosage," Dr. Stanton said.

Baine stared and tilted his head back as though the light from the ceiling would help his ability to stay alert.

"Baine?" Dr. Stanton said.

The snapping of Baine's head as he focused his attention toward Dr. Stanton caused a subtle flinch.

Dr. Stanton stared at his notepad.

"You'll help me stay awake?" Baine asked.

"I'll do my best," Dr. Stanton said.

"That's what Momma always says," Baine said.

"Who's Momma again?"

"Whatchu mean?"

"Baine, I want you to realize Momma is not real."

Baine shifted in his chair, sighed.

"You seem to have some kinda hate for my momma. You know she really doesn't like you much either, to be honest. Every time I tell her I'm comin' here she looks at me with evilness and then my grits have clumps and the eggs are cold. You ruin my breakfast, doc. All your questions and stuff; matter a fact I think I should stop takin' them pills you give me. They make her sense something in me and she has a great sixth sense, you know? It's like she can smell the medication comin' off my skin..."

That same smell fell over the room like mosquito netting. Dr. Stanton stood over the cup and stared until it became a blur and appeared as a painting. He loathed the moment he would have to explain how he missed Baine hinting defiance.

The night nurse gave that fake smile again.

"We notified the police of his escape," she said.

"How closely has the staff monitored my patient's medication?" asked Dr. Stanton.

"We keep detailed charts."

"Hmm...Look..."

He revealed the cup filled with pills.

The nurse covered her nose.

"My goodness," the nurse said. "They're from...?"

"Yeah, he hasn't been..."

"But I've watched him swallow them."

"Momma once told him not to take the pills, so I guess she's back at it again."

The nurse stared at the cup.

"Momma?"

"Yeah, he's been talking to her again somehow. That's why he came to New York."

"Funny, he told me he was here for a woman."

"Did he happen to tell you her name?"

"I think he said it was something like Sorita or maybe it was Sorenna."

"Sorena perhaps?"

"Maybe."

"I'm not getting anywhere," Dr. Stanton mumbled.

"Excuse me?"

"My patient, as you know, is schizophrenic."

"I know, but he talked about this woman so much I began believing she existed. To be honest, sir, I think that's why he left. He seemed as though he cared for her deeply."

Dr. Stanton thought of his wife smoking a cigarette.

"You think he left to find her?" the nurse asked.

"I'm sure he has but he's not safe out there, and without his medication…Who knows what'll happen in this town."

Dr. Stanton left the hospital with a tightening in his chest. *Anxiety*, he thought. *Not again.*

****

The New York air had thickened and there was a silence Stanton found eerie. The ground appeared swept and there was no smell of food or garbage or smog in the air. He considered his anxiety reached the point of euphoria and he already fainted inside and would later awaken inside the hospital in which he worked.

He glanced at his watch.

It was 9pm.

Thinking of his wife, he clutched the lining of his jacket to make sure he had not lost his phone during the confusion. He then pulled it out of his pocket, opened it, and dialed her number.

It rang twice.

"Hello?" her voice was a mere whisper.

"I'm sorry, honey. You were sleeping?"

"Yeah, long day. The wind took a tree down outside."

"Oh. Sorry. Well, I'll let you…"

"No, now you have to give me at least ten minutes of your voice."

Dr. Stanton smiled.

"A tree, huh?"

"Yeah, across the street; fell right on the road, didn't take down any powerlines though."

"That's good."

"So, you called to tell me your itinerary?"

"Actually, I called because I have some news."

"News, again?"

"My patient somehow escaped the mental hospital."

"Oh."

"I'm sorry. This is getting frustrating."

"For both of us, it seems."

"Yeah."

"What now? You have to stay?"

"Maybe. Not sure."

Dr. Stanton could tell his wife removed herself from the bed. He imagined her walking toward the window, peering at the tree lying sprawled across the street.

"I miss you," his wife said, sighing.

"I know. I think I've done all I've could over the past decade with this patient."

"I thought you were making progress."

"That's what I thought, but he seems to have another imaginary person that I was unaware of. This one may be a love interest which I think led him here to New York."

"He must really love this woman."

"I think he does."

He knew what she meant. He wanted to hear her say the words "come home". He wanted her to fight but he had already analyzed her as passive-aggressive in nature, and there would be no fight or argument or anything obvious.

Dr. Stanton stood silent, breathing against the New York breeze and the sound of his wife moving throughout the house. He thought he heard her opening the pack of cigarettes he hoped she wouldn't find.

"Well, gotta catch a train uptown," Dr. Stanton said. "You get some rest."

"I hope to. Another storm is coming," his wife said.

"I'll call you tomorrow and give you hopefully some better news."

"Okay, goodnight. I love you."

"Love you too."

****

Sorena finished the book over coffee and idle stares from Dean. Looking across the living room in her apartment she could still see the steam coming from the shower he had just taken.

"What're you looking at?" Sorena said, playfully.

"You think I might be depressed?" Dean asked.

"Maybe just homesick..."

Sorena picked the book up from the table, twirled it in her hand. "Thank you for this," she said.

Dean waved his hand. "No problem," he said. "You find this writer you're so in love with yet?"

Sorena shook her head.

"No, I haven't, and no, you're not depressed."

"I feel different though, like my body has expired."

"Stop drinking. I have noticed you don't drink much water."

"I'm a former New Yorker, have you seen the water? It's not exactly clear, you know?"

"You sound like a character from a Woody Allen film."

Dean smiled.

"I'm thinking I need to come back."

"No, you've moved up, don't!"

"I miss seeing you."

Sorena didn't want to hear this; she walked over toward the window in her living room and looked down toward the street. She could see a cab as it drove by slowly. She wanted to run outside, hail it, and get inside.

"You always do this," Sorena said.

"Do what?" Dean asked.

"Tell me you miss me or love me when I show interest in another man."

"I see you're still drunk. Yeah, maybe we shouldn't drink."

"I'm serious."

"Me too."

"Me too? None of what you're saying is true. Plus, it was me that told you to meet this man. Remember that?"

Sorena nodded.

Another cab went by.

"You hungry?"

Dean didn't respond.

There was quietness in the room. Dean removed himself from the couch and walked toward the bathroom. Sorena turned away from the window and began remembering the last letter she received from the strange man.

****

Baine entered the foyer of his apartment building. The security guard stared at him as though his face had begun melting. *I wonder if he can see Cyrano too*, he thought.

The security guard was an armed one. His mustache twitched, and his nostrils flared. He removed his hat and revealed a bald spot atop his head.

"Mr. Adams?"

"Uh, yeah?"

"Haven't seen you in a while, how are things?"

Baine considered this a trap.

"Away on a book tour," Baine said. "I didn't tell you?"

"Of course you didn't tell him, you idiot," Cyrano said. "Because it was me that wrote that book of yours; wait til Sorena finds out you're a complete hack. Oh, and the letters too. Don't forget about those."

"Shut up!" Baine mumbled.

"Excuse me, Mr. Adams?" the security guard said.

"Oh, nothing. Sorry. He's not minding his business."

"Who?"

"Cy."

"Oh."

The security guard was already reaching for the phone. He picked up his hat and placed it carefully atop his head.

"He's on to us," Cyrano uttered.

Baine walked quickly toward the elevator. Looking back would give away all the lies he covered. The untruths would spill from his eyes in rage scented by a dying entity that lingered within, one he wanted to keep alive so desperately.

He pressed the button for the elevator.

The security guard was on the phone, glancing in Baine's direction and seeming to whisper on the phone.

The elevator arrived. The doors slid apart. There stood a family, a nice looking one. So nice they appeared to be tourists from the Midwest: a white mother and father, well-matched for each other with dark hair and brown eyes and amiable grins, a small child, the same features. They were so perfect Baine stood silent as they exited. He watched them walk toward the door and wondered if he knew them.

He reached in his pocket, yanked the Moleskine from its place, wrote: IF PERFECTION HAD A FAMILY IT WOULD BE THE FAMILY I JUST SAW ON THE ELEVATOR.

****

Conchetta Violet had not come up in discussion with Baine, and Dr. Stanton could not locate his notes as to why her identity had disappeared. She was a nice girl, calm and perceptive, with a voice that eased Stanton's anxiety about being confined to his office for long hours. He often craved her presence. With guilt, he often adjusted the temperature in his office to bring her about. But somehow Baine kept her locked away in his mind, just as he had done with Cyrano.

"Perhaps that's why he came north..." Dr. Stanton mumbled to himself. "I wonder what this new identity is like, what she means to him..."

Dr. Stanton developed an image of Sorena in his mind: a tall, mysterious lady with brown skin and eyes the same, a smile wide and mischievous. He was on a subway platform taking in the view of all the ladies surrounding him.

Cyrano stood in the corner, his fading existence highlighted by the swatch of incoming light from the window. Baine, quiet and listening to his own breath, thought he could hear Cyrano's heart beating violently against the sounds of New York. "You need to leave," Baine mumbled.

Cyrano ignored him.

The air in the apartment had cooled. Baine had not realized he had succumbed to shivering until he attempted to speak again. "Ple-ase-g-go…"

"I have one more letter to write," Cyrano said.

"No…n…don't. I can—"

"-You won't do anything," Cyrano yelled. "You'll let her die like you did the others…!"

"What are you talking about?"

"You love from afar, never close enough to feel or smell the truth…Love doesn't exist."

Baine walked away from the living room. Sauntering toward the kitchen, he thought of ways he could end Cyrano's existence.

From the next room, he could hear Cyrano's bones cracking.

"I'll give you a chance to write your way out of my head for good," Baine said.

"You need me," said Cyrano.

"I need you to leave so I can have Sorena for myself."

Mumbled recitation of longing echoed across the room. Cyrano was now by the window, his deteriorating existence highlighted by the afternoon sun. His thinned outline made him look like an ailing insect; a weakened and desperate exoskeleton was reduced to moans and the clicking sound of his skeletal feet scraping across hardwood floors. Baine, now away from the kitchen, came upon a great sadness as he watched Cyrano wither. "You can't die alone," Baine said. "Grandpa died alone and drunk and that's not a proper way to meet heaven."

Baine turned away, stifled tears and looked about his apartment, which he had not noticed was bare and void of anything that revealed the life of a man with a successful life in letters. The walls were empty, and the corners of rooms were filled with grayish dust from Cyrano's decay. Crumpled letters were strewn about like giant blood-speckled popcorn kernels, marked up with red ink by relentless editing.

"I'm alone now…" Baine whispered.

He thought of the death of Conchetta, how her demise was quite similar. She had betrayed his heart, faded upon the air like mist never to return. "Let's talk about Conchetta," Dr. Stanton said, eyes full of inquisition. "She's gone," Baine would say, and it was all he wanted to say during those sessions. Talking about her burned like uninhibited sips of Grandpa's whiskey. There's was never the warm and comfort of inebriation, only the burn, as if Conchetta's soul was liquefied.

"I got rid of her."

"You acknowledge she was just a part of your mind?"

"She was real."

"Your trauma from abandonment is what's real," Baine.

Interruption of this moment was halted by a knock at the door.

"Hello…?"

Baine looked toward the window. It was long before he exited toward the fire escape.

O

Dr. Stanton thought the security guard looked like the son he never had. The guard's face was boyishly soft and bordered unblemished. The guard behind the desk just days before was not there, and the guard before him did not seem interested in Dr. Stanton's inquisition.

"No idea who this is," the guard said, scanning a photo Dr. Stanton handed him as though it were alive.

"He has a condition," Stanton said.

"A condition?"

"Has he ever appeared different to you…"

"Not sure what—"

"His personality."

"Dr. Stanton, is everything okay?"

"Yes, everything is…why do you ask?"

"I'm new here," the boyish guard began. "But I'm sure this man does not stay in this building."

Stanton recalled the agoraphobia. He had recorded this behavior during the summer of 1997 when it was discovered Baine had not left his boarding room in nearly a month. Upon discovering this, Stanton was stunned Baine had managed to live as seven different personalities to fence off feelings of loneliness. Most prominent were the personalities of Reginald, Uncle Pop, and Dexter. Reginald was a jokester, the most light-hearted of the three. He liked to sketch caricatures of Baine's friends. Always good for an ill-timed joke and a wandering pencil that captured the gangly features of southern boys and girls running about in the summer, Dexter often scolded Reginald for his efforts. "You know I'ont nothin' like that"! Dexter would say with a squeal.

"Your head is big, bigger than you think. I been tellin' you this since you came here," Reginald drawled, his pencil scraping across the page as he grinned like a mad scientist.

"Best to get me right if you gon' sit there and draw me," said Dexter.

Reginald never gave in. He'd continue: the pencil whisping delicately across the page, scraping, making shapes, intricate features, the drawing of imaginary presence.

Stanton left without going further with the security guard. He imagined him as too young and void of empathy to realize Baine's affliction. He was already back on the A, heading north in Manhattan, watching New Yorkers and thinking of his wife. He thought of their first time together in the city and how at that time, her being with him made the city feel more alive. The lights in the subway tunnel as the train went by, the glowing, rhythmic glare that danced steadily in his wife's eyes along with the sound of the tracks beneath. The bouncing of the train made her lean against him and how her body felt warm and comfortable. Her smile, sincere and warm as her person, confirmed her love. He would feel this forever and things would never change. There was no naivete to elude the rush of passion, nothing unsure or full of doubt. His love was amplified by the sights and sounds of a city passing above.

****

Back in his hotel room, Stanton dialed his home phone.

"Hello," his wife answered. Her breath was heavy.

"Just get in?" Stanton asked.

"Run was brutal this morning."

"At least you braved it."

Stanton's wife would run only during times of stress. Over the years she had grown sporadic in her efforts to de-stress by exercise.

"Everything okay?" Stanton inquired.

There was silence.

Listening closely to the sounds of suburban Atlanta, the sounds that placed him in the kitchen in his home, his arms wrapped around his wife's waist that was no longer thin but still as wonderful as Stanton remembered. "I'm fine," she said. "How are things in New York?"

"Baine is hard to find here."

"Are the local police helping?"

"Not sure I want to involve them again."

"Good thing he's not a threat to other people."

"Might be easier if he was though, I hate to say."

****

Sorena's new nightmare started with a newspaper headline: ESCAPED ATLANTA PSYCHIATRIC HOSPITAL PATIENT BELIEVED TO BE IN NEW YORK...

Closing the paper, she gave in to a long stare across the room. Often, she kept her living room bathed in ambient light that in this instance seemed to glow darker than she remembered. On the table, highlighted by the glow of a standing lamp near her window, *The Cornbread Diaries* loomed. The book she had become engrossed in with, words that conveyed every longing she had ever experienced in life, lay within the evening silence, its title sideways and taunting her. The dreams she carried with her to bed induced by wondrous prose that leaped from the pages and formed itself in front of her eyes on many nights, had now perhaps been written by a man not clear in thought, not clear in his reality that intrigued her that day on the train. She crafted a memory of him, his face soft and sincere and rather unblemished, and his voice calm and soothing; was this man real or consumed by traits of someone developed from his condition? *The one man in this city I meet that's charming and doesn't smell like street meat and cheap wine and he's an escaped mental patient?* Sorena thought to herself.

Opening the book that evening, under the soft light emitting from the lamp on her nightstand, the pages felt heavier. The letters appeared larger. Despite this, her reading was the same; her curiosity now heightened because the fear had subsided and now it was time to investigate further, further for her sanity to remain whole. *This book still speaks to me*, she thought. And she wondered how it spoke to others.

120

She wondered if the letters she received were circulated to other women across the island of Manhattan. Selfishly, and because there were days she wanted her life to move in time like that of a romantic comedy, she hoped she was the lone receiver of the letters she read at night.

The city sounds had dissipated under her thoughts. She had forgotten the time and found her eyes growing heavy. The pages, blurred and repeating in her mind, aided her to sleep. She was no longer scared; she was longing for the man she met that day on the train. She wanted him to show his face again, to smile that shy smile and speak to her in his slow, syrupy southern dialect and for his thoughts and poetic musings to leave her open and ready for his next arrival.

****

Stanton sat quietly in one of the smallest bookstores in New York City known as 3Lives and Company. On a corner of 154 West 10th Street, it was a place he assumed Baine would feel welcomed as he shut off his investigative mind and absorbed the surroundings—taking in the smell of new and old books and over-brewed coffee. New York moved at its usual pace outside but the calm within the bookstore brought Stanton south, where home was quiet and joined by sounds of the planet and not sounds of industry and anger. Atlanta's inner city was just as busy in sections, but the overwhelming pace was escapable in New York.

Extracting his hand-held tape recorder from the inside pocket on his light jacket, he began quietly recording…

This place reminds me of the quietest part of my study, the part away from the window that faces the street where I can see the skyline of

Buckhead. Outside from where I sit looks like a movie, people and activity and I can't help but wonder if among them, Baine is in the same place watching and writing about their movements just as I am here recording them verbally. I'm not even sure of what I'll do if I find him again. In all my years of psychotherapy with many complex and imprisoned minds, I wonder if Baine's writing this book is indeed his moment, his breakthrough—but I hate the term breakthrough, as it implies there were walls in the first place and Baine's mind is indeed unlocked...it's just he has a lot of different doors...

Dr. Stanton's documentation was interrupted by a woman walking past the bookstore. Her free hand clutching the handlebar of a stroller, the other with a cellphone pressed against her ear. Her dark hair was wild, windblown, and swept back far enough to reveal the protrusion of veins running the length of her forehead. Her eyes, blue and glassed over, were wide as though fearful of the world before her. Stanton sat back in his chair and watched her spastic mannerisms. She turned the corner to disappear toward the teeming throng of Manhattanites and it was then a most horrible discovery came to Dr. Stanton. *The baby stroller's empty*, he thought. *Where is she...*

Before Baine, Stanton had never followed anyone before. But curiosity had bested his efforts to stay within the confines of the bookstore. *I too must be losing my mind,* he thought. There was a moment where he thought the woman had spotted him. At a crosswalk, it seemed she was on to something. She turned, eyes still wide and full of fear. Craving a moment of conversation with the mysterious woman, Dr. Stanton could only watch her, could only dart his eyes in the direction of the empty baby stroller, which upon closer examination revealed it was filled to the edges with National Geographic magazines.

"...Her cellphone," he began mumbling to himself, "It's...deactivated..."

Before he could call out to the woman the light had changed and the crosswalk became cluttered with people walking back and forth. *She's gone*, he thought. And she was lost within the sea of people.

Later it occurred to Dr. Stanton he perhaps came upon a moment of hallucination. Lack of sleep and stress had seemed to consume him as he tracked Baine's existence. Seemed he could only now take sessions with Baine through *The Cornbread Diaries*.

Carefully he leafed through the pages, scanning them as he did previously, searching for keywords that gave hints to location, feelings, and thoughts hidden deep within. But he wasn't ready to fully take in the beauty before him. He had only studied and researched Baines affliction, only knew of him through their sessions together. What his eyes had taken in during his careful reading of the first five pages stunned him to pause.

"It's all here..." he said to himself. It was clear Baine's breakthrough had come in the form of writing. The voice was unlike anything Stanton had heard before. It was clear, sharp, resonant, and full of wit and confidence.

He stopped reading for a moment, mused about his hotel room while every so often looking steadily out over the clean vista of the Manhattan street. He wondered where Baine was and what personality bestowed him in the moment, the moment under the night sky and fervor of New York City. The prose had startled Dr. Stanton to a revelation that was

123

not clear as he scurried about the city. It had occurred to him he had grown emotionally weary, as missing his wife and worrying of her safety and love for him consumed his analytical mind. Inside the pages of Baine's masterpiece, he was able to hide from the world and escape for a moment. He only stopped to mull over a striking sentence about a woman, a woman he faintly remembered Baine mention during one of their sessions. The mentioning of her was more striking and palpable in the book. There were details Baine had left out during their session. In the writing, Stanton came across a clear sense of her as though she was standing in the room. He could smell her scent. Other details alluded to changes Stanton found surprising. So much that a revelation came upon him that woke him from sleep.

Has Baine created a new personality, that of a woman? Is that why he came north? Further examination of this original thought flipped itself, changed form and showed Stanton things that felt positive and resonant. *If the woman is real, he has come to make a connection...*

A REAL CONNECTION.

Stanton grabbed his hand-held tape recorder:

"A...breakthrough...progress...Baine is trying to connect to people...things...outside of what he's created in his mind. This book—although perhaps written by one of his other personalities—is the story of this longing to heal his fragmented mind. This isn't just an escape of the mind it is an escape, a rebirth of sorts, of the soul...

"...He's living through the act of writing..."

Stanton stopped recording. He had only once before came upon such revelations in his most complex cases but this one arrived upon the wind of a city full with distractions and confusion, came to him as he missed his wife and the life he felt as though he left behind to get lost searching for answers he'd never find. And for this, Stanton hoped there was truth in his theory. In the quiet that consumed his mind, he allowed the thought to remain safe, unhindered. And for the first time since arriving in New York

He felt his purpose fulfilled.

****

Sorena found what she assumed was a letter she had forgotten to read. Standing in the muted quiet of her apartment she searched all over for the letter's original envelope but came across nothing of the sort as she tried to remember dates and times when she last saw the man on the train known to her as Baine. Her heart and mind had already come to know his words in ways that made her blush and feel desired like she had not since the awful days of online. She so wanted to feel Baine's voice caressing the deepest most forbidden parts of her body as she scurried about her dwelling, rooting through boxes and piles of junk mail. *This tonight*, she thought. *This will consume me...*

The letter was thick, approached a length of ten pages. Some of the ink smeared slightly, enlivened the mystery of where Baine perhaps sat to compose. She imagined him tucked in a dark corner at a café, a dark, stiff cocktail—brown in color—accompanying his feverish writing and his heart racing as he came across the words that found a home inside his mind full of whimsy and romanticism that brought him to New York. There would be no interrupting this moment, no idle chit chat with patrons nearby. This was a moment that required the recording of feelings, indescribable feelings. Feelings consumed by both lust and wonder and intrigue. Feelings embedded in one's soul and bones, ones with the consistency no one could possibly remove with jealousy or malice. It was pure and engrained, these longings deep within like marrow made of things that moved one to tears and unrivaled happiness.

Sorena was no longer embarrassed by these feelings for a writer she met. She felt comforted in the allowance.

"I was sure you could only ever love me," Dean said, playfully. "You like this Baine?"

"I know I shouldn't, but I do," said Sorena.

"What next?"

"Next?"

"Yes, with this guy."

She paused.

"I like his writing."

"But you met him so maybe there's a chance…"

"Stop."

"Stop?"

"You're not suggesting…"

"Hell yes I am!"

They laughed for a little while, laughed like they used to as kids. But within the joy and connection they often shared effortlessly with one another, Sorena did not want to give in easily to Dean's gentle accusation of her longing. She recalled how fun it was for her to be teased by Dean when he knew she was interested in someone. And the memory of those gentle moments comforted her.

"You know me so well," Sorena said, wishing Dean was there with her and they were on their second bottle of wine.

"I never want you to be without the kind of love I have for you," Dean said, gently. "Even if it's from someone damaged," he added.

"Aren't we all walking around these cities damaged," Sorena asked, rhetorically.

"Yes, but some of us deny ourselves the love we deserve," Dean replied.

And it soon came to Sorena like the breeze coming in from the city before her. Had she denied herself love all these years because fate would have her on the A heading north beneath the bustle and teeming world of Manhattan? Was the writer of the book she had grown to love perhaps in no way connected to the man she met on the train? Was there now a choice to be made and which one was best? Was she hoping all those years Dean was the one and his preference for men was merely a phase, and each man Dean spoke of was merely a stand-alone piece of everything that existed in her?

Later Sorena compiled all the letters and found a place to read on the stoop outside of her building. Evening was approaching and the setting sun in the distance infiltrated the pristine vista of her street with ambient, romantic light, just enough to add to feelings she had not felt since the first time she longed for someone. Transported back to early autumns in Queens, she regained a sense of being desired again, but not for her looks, more for her whole being, her energy and aura, her voice and things unseen by men only in tune with her glowing skin, dark hair mand lips shaped perfectly below her symmetrical nose and eyes. The letters erased the moments of catcalling by eager, less than regal men, the eyes of hungry wanderers on the A train that ran late into the night from Brooklyn. It erased the worry of late-night walks through Central Park, the haunting memory of being followed home by a homeless man that swore he only needed money for food but held within his eyes a hunger Sorena could only think was for her body. The letters erased all the mental soot of things dirty and unwanted and gave her the world in soft, muted shades, like old movies and aged photographs of men and women in love. And this feeling— this moment—lasted for the remainder of an evening no longer filled with questions; it was now filled with purpose: to find the man that penned the words that helped her see the gleaming underside of humanity and that love was possible in a loveless city slightly torn by terrorism.

Sorena read the first few lines that started her longing:

Since my arrival to the city I have thought of you often; I have imagined your presence on the subway heading north toward uptown. From our meeting, I have not been able to pull my eyes away from the remaining burn in my psyche left by your powerful brightness…

"And there you are," Baine began. "A pile of ashes lying before the city I've grown to love. Await the breeze, my friend. Await the breeze. Soon, you'll be happily dispersed; a distant memory. I'll finally be able to live as my true self."

Baine thought he heard Cyrano utter one last word before a gentle breeze sent the remains across the Hudson River. Off in the wind, Cyrano sailed. Baine would live by Cyrano's words no longer. His energy and presence was weakened by Baine's need to connect with a world he created.

Walking away from the river, his first thought without the saddling cynicism of Cyrano was if he could pen letters as himself that were as rich; letters honest and from the soul like the ones he penned for Violet as a child. Thoughts of composing while capturing the wind from the steel mill in Pipeshop under that willow tree overlooking the creek momentarily replaced the concrete of New York surrounding him. But as strong as this vision developed, so remained the dust of Cyrano's bones, which Baine knew would at times emit echoed remnants of thoughts that hindered him to write

129

as himself. *How can I explain to the world the great* The Cornbread Diaries *were written not as me but as the man I just murdered?* Baine thought. *I hope he never returns. I hope I'm strong enough.*

The C train was empty. "Keep away from the closing doors, please…" That familiar command reminded Baine of the first time he saw Sorena. He was glad it was not rush hour. He did not want his imagination infiltrated by the view of a man sleeping nearby or a curmudgeonly old woman's face twisted upward by the disdain of youth surrounding her. With clarity before him, the train was only littered with a few dreary eyed passengers, for which he could watch and build stories from their existence. He was happy the unfiltered writer had returned. The absence of thoughts swayed from another entity was enough to induce a grin. Comfortable in this newfound contentment, he saw what was viewed previously by eyes hazed over by the pesky periphery of Cyrano. Before him was a new world, a beginning untouched by the dirt-tinged stroke of Cyrano's restless brush.

As the train rumbled southward below Manhattan, Baine extracted his journal from his pocket and begin to write:

It is on this day I am reborn. Cyrano has fallen as I knew he would someday. And for this, I am wholly grateful and feel my soul has lightened immensely. New York to me now is a new place. It is ripened and sweet and untouched. The Big Apple they call it. I shall sink my teeth into it.

He smiled as himself and did not feel he would have to explain a bit of it later. The new course had begun without hindrance and the next day he would pen a letter to Sorena himself. The dream of finding love would continue.

Recorded snippet of Phone Interview with Dr. Leo Grumbine for International Daily News, December 5th, 2002

Dr. Leo Grumbine's voice was thick, "We've been searching for Dr, Herman Stanton for some time now," he said.

"He's not Baine Adams?" the interviewer asked.

"I'm afraid that's one part of who Dr. Herman Stanton is…"

Dr. Herman Stanton—an accomplished writer and family man—disappeared from the Georgia State Mental Hospital during the summer of 1999.

Sorena stared at the report on the computer screen for what felt like hours. She read about the mysterious disappearance of Conchetta Violet, the theory of suicide or perhaps being murdered by Herman Stanton himself. "There's no way…" she mumbled. She could not erase the sweet memory of the man on the A train. She failed in dimming the light he rekindled in her soul. His words were too clear in her mind and heart. No way could the hands that crafted words and images so captivating be the hands of someone that had taken the life of his mother. But that's what Dr. Grumbine believed, and it is what the Atlanta Juvenile Justice System concluded: BY REASON OF INSANITY, THE STATE OF GEORGIA VS. HERMAN STANTON, THE SENTENCE OF LIFE AT THE GEORGIA STATE HOSPITAL SHALL BE APPOINTED…

Missing for many years, Dr. Stanton made imaginary calls to his wife, almost daily. It was told Mrs. Stanton had since moved to Europe and had remarried after accepting her husband's illness and that a life with him was something of the past. Sorena imagined how sad these calls must have been. In her visions of this moment of melancholy and confusion, she could see a pile of letters written under the other personalities of Dr. Stanton's other voice, the one that penned her great letters of love and wonder. Letters that explained how longing and love worked from inside out and how one day the serendipitous happenings that brought people together would change the world for the better and how 9/11 was that one singular event to make these moments more powerful and full of meaning. *I wonder what kind of woman she is*, Sorena thought. *Such patience and strength...*

Sorena wondered if she was able to have the same reserve; if she was able to just live in random moments of love, to await the next letter—or one day a phone call—from whomever Dr, Stanton was that day. Is this what she would find in a city of millions of men? Was this the kind of love she was destined for? The intangible yet fulfilling romanticism she had only witnessed in movies and what she once wanted from Dean before he came out as a gay man?

"I have something I need to tell you..." she recalled hearing Dean say as he awaited the A Local. *I don't want to hear what anyone must tell me*, Sorena thought. *I want to fucking feel it!*

Sorena listened to the recorded interview with Dr. Grumbine as everything around her began to seem like something from a dream.

Dr. Stanton's childhood journal was the subject, the letters he had written to his childhood friend, Conchetta Violet, the last real woman other than Momma that consumed his soul. "It's possible we can get to him through his writing," said Dr. Grumbine

"Should the public be worried?" the reporter asked.

"The public should only be concerned that a writer, a person, well...a doctor of Herman Stanton's caliber may perhaps be lost upon the world as he continues to search for his mother, who passed many years ago."

"Interesting, yet sad..."

"We need to get him back to Georgia as safely as possible."

"Again, with regard to my duty to keep things confidential, I will only say this: the only thing dangerous about Dr. Stanton is his ability to give in to his own imaginary lives."

The view from where Sorena sat most of her days in her apartment had suddenly changed. No longer was there a soft light entering through the window from the street; it had seemed to dim just as her hopes of New York romance. The uneasiness was accentuated by shadows and shapes presented by passing cars below as they went by beneath the hopeless glow. She sat and watch the curtains against the windows move, watched them dance from the wind's music as she imagined things both horrible and wondrous. She couldn't possibly tell Dean of this, as he would blame himself for aiding her toward the possibility of romance. All Sorena could do in the moment was think of the letters and their chance meeting, a meeting that dissolved all the other chance meetings she had with men in New York. It was nothing special, but the authenticity struck her. The nuances were different. Things moved slowly like the hands of a clock, but the progression was felt rather than watched.

She removed herself from where she sat and considered a stiff drink. *I'll need this before I talk to Dean,* she thought.

Later that day, Sorena read the letters carefully. She looked for clues, coded words, deeper meanings missed. But all she found were images that soothed and complimented, sang to her and made her feel calm and relaxed. Her imagination was too flooded with sensory to pull away from the discoveries that made her feel uneasy just hours before.

On the phone with Dean with letters placed intricately on her floor in the best chronological order she could muster, she said, "You may or may not believe what I'm about to tell you about that writer I met."

Dean was breathing heavily.

"I never believe anything about a writer in New York City."

"I'm serious."

"Serious enough to call me on my early morning run?"

"When did you start running?"

"When the last guy I went out with said something about my weight."

"Oh."

Sorena wanted to laugh but couldn't. She could only—for a moment—think of how Dean was changing. "Apparently the man I met is more than a writer," Sorena said.

There was a long silence.

"Uh... what?" Dean breathed.

"He's a shrink," Sorena said. "Well, he was..."

"Wait, wait…the writer you met on the subway? Are we talking about the same man?"

"The writer on the subway."

Sorena wished she could see Dean's face; his voice didn't coincide with her imagining his mouth open, eyes affixed on the shock of her statement as it lingered within the air and space they often shared.

"Who's the lovely man that's sending you all the letters?"

Dean didn't interject much as Sorena told him the man she thought was Baine Henry Adams was indeed Dr. Herman Stanton, a man afflicted with Dissociative Identity Disorder; a brilliant man that housed within his soul the actions and lives of beings both conflicted and detrimental. "His mother went missing when he was as a child," Sorena said, almost whispering it. To say such a thing aloud while sitting alone in her apartment felt like she would awaken a sadness she had not felt since her last time with Dean. The lingering entity of melancholy by words that arrived from the very man that brought words to life for her-was too much to think of in the moment.

"Are you okay there, by yourself?" Dean asked, calm and assured.

Sorena nodded, realizing she hadn't replied verbally. "Yes, yes…I…"

There was quiet on the other end. She could hear Dean sigh.

"You do realize he has your address."

Sorena looked over toward her door. On a normal day, the many passing shadows that slid beneath the miniscule opening from the bottom of her front door failed to elicit longing for the arrival of someone. This time, as a passing shadow eased by, void was her ability to dismiss it. "Are you there?" Dean asked. His voice was now filled with concern.

"You think…" Sorena began.

"…Yes, I'm thinking a lot of things from hearing this!" said Dean.

"I mean, do you think I'm someone real to him?"

"Why would he mistake all that you are as something not real?"

There was silence. Sorena loved how Dean always knew what to say, no matter how much it hurt or soothed.

"Why do you always have the right answers?" Sorena asked.

"Because, my dear, I've used up all the wrong ones."

■■

The cab smelled like old bread and cinnamon. Sorena could not remember the last time she sat inside one as an adult. The only memory she had of New York City cabs was from childhood, one of her and her mother on their way to a family member's funeral in Queens. The cab driver's eyes every few seconds glanced toward the back seat. His brown eyes seemed to say things about what life held before her, all the things that came and went and failed to make sense. Death was the beginning of this; such a surprise she didn't know anything about it until now.

On her lap sat the box of letters that made her feel whole and special again. Letters from a man whom she imagined would perhaps never grasp in his many minds the effect they had on her life.

"Nice day today," the cab driver said.

Sorena, lost in thoughts of a romance with words and thoughts that aided her through Dean's moving away, did not hear the cabbie. She looked up at the cabby's eyes, which had softened enough to hint inquiry. "I'm sorry, you said something?"

"Just it's a nice day today," the cab driver said. "You're lucky you get to enjoy it."

"Lucky?"

"Ma'am, I drive a lot of people all over this city and forgive my assumption, but you seem as though you're enjoying your life here in New York."

"What's not to enjoy?"

"Exactly. I mean, you read books? Yeah, I'm reading this book now written by a guy named Baine Adams, he talks about New York in this book the way my Grandparents did. They came over here from Italy in the 1800's; they were in love with each other and new possibilities and the day was nice, just like this. Makes you forget about what happened last year and all. You read this book? It's called *The Cornbread Diaries*, best book I've read in years. Makes you love New York all over again. And believe me we all know how much love this city needs after what happened to those people in the towers, D.C., and Pennsylvania."

Sorena could only smile and nod. "I've heard of that book," she said. "Sounds like something I'd love to read.

The cab driver pulled away from the corner of 180 Greenwich Street driving off into the stately Manhattan vista amongst a sea of yellow steel on wheels. Sorena, with a box of letters in hand, walked toward Ground Zero with eyes glassy from emotion but filled with hope. She didn't need Dean to love her like she wanted. She didn't need him to come back to New York and confess his love her. All she had hoped for came in the form of a man searching for what was real in a dented city filled with people all looking for a sense of hope. Love still existed, and it existed in the book and letters and written by Dr. Herman S. Stanton aka Baine Henry Adams aka Cyrano.

A letter written in the voice of Baine Adams composed by Dr. Herman S. Stanton during the summer of 2018, in an undisclosed location somewhere in the United States:

Dear people of the city I call home:

I write this to you upon the grand unveiling of the September 11th Memorial in Lower Manhattan. It was with great joy that I express my most sincere adulation toward your recovery and display of strength. Seems the dust is gone. The cries for help no longer heard within the rubble created from hate. Love has returned to the greatest place on Earth and for that, I am glad I was able to touch the lives of a few by writing of my love for the greatest city in the world.

Sincerely…